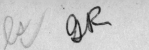

"Lucy, Allen is downstairs!" Momma called up.

She sighed and tossed a bed pillow. *Oh please, not now.* "I have a headache!" she called back. It was true. Already she felt the tension creeping up her neck and into the back of her head from her emotional turmoil. After a few anxious minutes, she heard the front door shut, then footsteps on the stairs. The door to her room opened a crack.

"Really, Lucy," Momma admonished, handing her a note. "I don't know what's gotten into you. Do you really have a headache or is something else bothering you?"

"I don't know, Momma. Thank you for bringing me the note."

Momma gave her one last look before heading down the stairs. Lucy unfolded the paper and read Allen's message—which included many misspellings. It said he would be in Elkins for a week and when he returned, to be ready for a wonderful night out to finish what they had started today. She refolded the note and set it on the lamp table. *What is it we're supposed to finish, Allen?* she thought. *Have we really started anything? I mean, I like you and all. We've been friends since we learned to talk. But are we really supposed to be together? Am I supposed to be your girl? Even marry you? Or should we just stay friends?*

Lucy began to shiver again like she had back at the river. Only then did she realize she was still wearing her wet overalls. When she stood up, a damp impression remained on the bedspread. *Now I am losing my mind. But why? Can it all be because of those soldiers we met in the fields today, and especially one named Captain Nick Landers?*

LAURALEE BLISS, a former nurse, is a prolific writer of inspirational fiction, as well as a home educator. She resides with her family near Charlottesville, Virginia, in the foothills of the Blue Ridge Mountains—a place of inspiration for many of her contemporary and historical novels. Lauralee writes inspirational fiction to provide readers with entertaining stories, intertwined with Christian principles to assist them in their day-to-day walk with the Lord. Aside from writing, she enjoys gardening, cross-stitching, reading, roaming yard sales, and traveling. Lauralee invites you to visit her Web site at www.lauraleebliss.com.

Books by Lauralee Bliss

HEARTSONG PRESENTS

HP249—Mountaintop
HP333—Behind the Mask
HP457—A Rose Among Thorns
HP538—A Storybook Finish
HP569—Ageless Love
HP622—Time Will Tell
HP681—The Wish
HP695—Into the Deep
HP755—Journey to Love

Don't miss out on any of our super romances. Write to us at the following address for information on our newest releases and club information.

Heartsong Presents Readers' Service
PO Box 721
Uhrichsville, OH 44683

Or visit www.heartsongpresents.com

Seneca
Shadows

Lauralee Bliss

Heartsong Presents

To my father-in-law, Ken Bliss, with grateful thanks for his wisdom, his prayers, and his service to our country.

A note from the Author:
I love to hear from my readers! You may correspond with me by writing:

Lauralee Bliss
Author Relations
PO Box 721
Uhrichsville, OH 44683

ISBN 978-1-59789-781-5

SENECA SHADOWS

Our mission is to publish and distribute inspirational products offering exceptional value and biblical encouragement to the masses.

PRINTED IN THE U.S.A.

one

Summer 1943

The gentle rush of the North Fork River played a soothing melody to Lucy Bland. She tucked a section of hair behind one ear and tentatively took a few steps forward, hoping her sneakers wouldn't slip on the wet rocks.

"Watch yourself there, Lucy!" a voice called out. "I was out here just a few days ago and the river nearly carried me off."

Lucy sighed. *Oh, to be carried away,* she thought. But not by a wild river rapid that came on the heels of some terrific thunderstorm. She had seen the valley drowned by rising waters. It often happened in the springtime with the melting snows and the onslaught of rainy weather. When the fields became engulfed by water, her family would seek her uncle's farm to pasture the horses and cattle.

No, not carried away by the river, but to be swept away by a man, safe in his strong arms—that was a different story. He would place her on his white steed and take her to his castle in the sky. What a wonderful romantic tale that would make. If only it would come true. She glanced back while teetering precariously on a rock with the river dancing at her feet. Her prince of the field was approaching her now. Short. Stocky. His red hair ignited by the fierce sunlight. He wore a brown shirt and stained trousers that had seen better days. Allen Hopper, the childhood friend she had known as far back as she could remember, the same one who used to steal her sweater at recess and her apple at lunch. Was he the person she longed for, her knight in shining armor?

"What are you doing, Lucy?" he demanded. "I said I had to talk to you about something important, and you take off on me."

"I want to cross the river, Allen," she said. "Let's go up in the woods across the way, toward my favorite place by the rocks. I just love the view from up there. It's so beautiful."

Allen shielded his eyes to glance at the famous rocks hovering above them, like pointed sentinels standing guard over the valley. "We're going way up there?" he complained.

She took another hop forward on the rock. How could she tell him that up there, among the pointy rocks, with the valley spread out before her, she felt as if she could touch heaven? Especially when clouds enshrouded the land.

"C'mon, don't do that." He came to the bank. "Am I gonna have to come in there after you?"

Lucy giggled at the thought. Maybe there were ways to make one's dream of being carried off to some distant land a reality. Momma often told her that her head lay more in the clouds than in the real world. Lucy admitted that sometimes she thought of the rocks as some great castle and herself as the queen of the gate. Some time ago, her younger brothers once caught her pretending to be a regal woman before the mirror.

"What are you doing, Lucy, acting dumb?" they had chided. As if to say she couldn't be anyone else but Lucy Bland, as bland and boring as her name.

Just then she felt a hand brush hers. Startled at the sudden touch, she screamed as she lurched away and slipped on the rock, landing on her knees in the rushing water. The chill shocked her, and she drew in a sharp breath. "Oh, now look at what you did!"

"I'm sorry, Lucy, but I told you to come out of there. I have something important to tell you."

She accepted his hand and slowly made her way back to the riverbank. Her overalls felt like they weighed a ton after the mishap in the river. She began to shake from the heavy, cold fabric against her skin.

"If you're cold, I'll give you my shirt," Allen said, starting to unbutton it.

Just the thought of seeing him without his shirt on made her blush. "No, no, I'll be fine," she managed to say. "It's my overalls that are wet. I'd better go home and change."

Allen blew out a sigh of dismay. "When are we ever gonna have some peace to ourselves, Lucy? Am I gonna have to kidnap you or something to get some time alone with you? There's always something that keeps us apart."

Kidnapped and carried off. She couldn't help but smile until she saw the look of irritation on his face. "I'm sorry, Allen. I guess I need to. . ."

Just then she heard a roar echo in the valley, bouncing between the two ridges of mountains that flanked them on either side. She glanced upward to see a perfectly blue sky without a hint of clouds. It couldn't be a storm brewing. Then she saw a procession of olive green trucks rumbling down the main road running through the valley. One of the trucks veered off the road and headed into the field, directly toward her and Allen.

"C'mon," Allen urged, taking her by the hand. Her sopping wet clothing did little to help her move any quicker. The roar of the truck grew deafening. Its brakes suddenly squealed and the truck came to a halt. The acrid stench of exhaust filled her nostrils.

"No need to be afraid," announced a friendly voice. From out of the truck came two men dressed in olive green fatigues and caps.

Lucy stared. "Oh, no," she whispered and found herself stepping toward Allen for protection.

"What's going on here?" Allen demanded. "Why are you driving on this land?"

"Don't mean to alarm you," the man said. He offered his hand. "I'm Captain Nick Landers. And this is Sergeant Fred Watkins. We're with the MTG."

"The what?" Allen asked.

"The MTG. Sorry. It stands for Mountain Training Group. We're out of Camp Hale, Colorado."

"Never heard of it—or you, for that matter."

Lucy continued to stare at the soldiers standing before her, from the top of the olive green caps on their heads, to the uniforms they wore, to the military boots that clad their feet. What could the military possibly want in this part of the valley? "I never thought I looked like a German," Lucy suddenly remarked. "In fact, my family has English roots."

Loud laughter emanated from the man who had introduced himself as Captain Nick Landers. "I'm sure," he said. "Though if you were German, you'd be the prettiest one in the East."

Lucy felt the heat enter her cheeks as Allen's hand tightened around her arm. "What do you want here, soldier?" Allen asked.

"Didn't you hear the news? The military has set up a base of operations in this part of West Virginia. We have men here that have already established a climbing school over in

Elkins. My job is to train groups of soldiers to climb those rocks there." He pointed toward Lucy's beloved castle in the distance.

"You mean you're going to climb Seneca Rocks?" Lucy asked in disbelief.

"That and much more. At least we will be training in that general area. There are divisions in different regions that will be doing other types of training maneuvers like working with artillery. The sergeant here and I came early to scout the area for the best place to set up a base camp from where the soldiers can begin climbing exercises." He gestured toward the green fields beyond. "And this looks like an excellent place. By the end of the week you'll see tents scattered all over this field."

Lucy wasn't sure she liked the prospect of strange men running around the valley and invading her beloved rocks. Though she had to admit she did like Nick's smile, and his laughter nearly made her laugh with him.

"Well, this is my family's field. Who gave you permission to trespass on our property and set up a bunch of tents?" Allen demanded.

Nick stared at him. "He's called Uncle Sam. The military selected this location because of its topography; it's ideal for training troops for conditions in Europe. Climbing studs set in a wall wouldn't give our troops the invaluable practice on the type of real terrain we expect to encounter in battle. Maybe we can even encourage you to enlist and help us with our training, Mister. . ."

"Hopper. Allen Hopper. My family owns a good deal of the land here. And the only country store in these parts, too. And I will tell you right now, my dad never said anything about you military men coming here and invading our land. Or driving your truck across it. Look at how you dug it up." He pointed at the deep tire tracks made in the soft ground.

"You might want to ask him again. We sent out maneuver permission cards about our plans. They alerted folks here about what we are doing and how long we'll be staying. Cards were sent to other places, as well, where other training will be conducted. And I'm sure good, upstanding citizens like yourselves believe that anything to help give us victory is worth a little inconvenience and some tire tracks, don't you think?"

Lucy could feel the tension rising out of this encounter. She tugged on Allen's hand. "Let's go, Allen. They have to do what they have to do. There's no sense arguing about it. I need to change into some dry clothes."

"There's plenty of other places they can do their training, like those rocks north of here," he muttered. "They'll only end up leaving this place a mess. I'm gonna talk to Dad about this and see what's going on."

Lucy glanced back at the two men who were already retracing their steps toward their truck. Suddenly Captain Landers paused, turned, and gave her one last once-over. She thought she saw the crease of a smile break his smoothly shaven face. Why would he be smiling at her? Maybe he found her humorous. Plenty of city people had come through the valley, looking on the residents here as simple-minded country folk. She lifted her head and turned away, linking her arm with Allen's. Again she thought she heard Nick's infectious laugher, but only the sound of the truck's engine revving up met her ears. Exhaust blew on the wind, replacing the sweet scent of flowers and green grass with the odor of oil.

Allen took off his hat and fanned away the fumes, coughing

all the while. "I'm gonna find out what's happening, all right," he declared, watching the truck make a U-turn and head for the road. "Just look at how those truck tires tore up the ground. And with a bunch of men camping here, this place will never be the same. How are we gonna graze our livestock?"

"Nothing is the same since Pearl Harbor," Lucy mused. "All Daddy talks about is the war. You hear it on the radio or at the picture shows. And all those men dying. It's awful." She glanced back wistfully as the truck disappeared into the distance. "Maybe it's a good idea to let them do what they want, Allen. I mean, we're helping the war effort, like that captain said."

"We're already helping the war effort. Dad sells war bonds at the store. And we've started rationing."

"Momma just got a ration book for sugar, too. She says we can't use sugar like we used to. And that means I can't make muffins anytime I want."

"I can get you all the sugar you need and you know it," Allen said. "So you keep on making your muffins."

"Yes, but that's not being honest, Allen. So many others can't have it. Momma says we need to do our part and use the coupons. Just like everyone else."

"Yeah, Dad's even gotten involved in that training to become one of those air raid wardens. Not that we would ever get bombs dropping on us here, of all places." He paused. "Though with those soldiers running around, who knows what could happen? They may drop their own bombs on us from the looks of it."

"Don't say those things, Allen. You're scaring me. They're just here to train on the rocks. And we should help them feel at home."

Allen fell silent. Lucy wasn't certain why he reacted the way he did toward the soldiers. Maybe the fact that he hadn't joined the army like others his age had left him with a guilty conscience. His father had been able to keep him from enlisting, claiming a need for Allen's help at the store. Not that she wanted Allen to join the army. No one knew what the future held or when the government would send troops into harm's way to drive out the enemy. Even though the war still seemed a long way away from West Virginia, the sights and sounds on the radio and on the newsreels made it real. Now, with soldiers arriving in Seneca Rocks, the war had come directly to their front doorstep. Lucy trembled despite the warm summer temperatures, more from nerves than her wet overalls.

When they reached her home, Allen turned and took her hand in his. "I still need to talk to you about something important," he said. "But I guess this isn't the time or the place. You need to get into some dry clothes."

"I'm sorry it didn't work out today, Allen."

He sighed. "It's all right. I have to get ready to go on a business trip to Elkins for Dad. When I get back, I'll take you to Petersburg for an ice-cream soda and we'll talk then. How does that sound?"

"Sounds real nice," she said with a smile. He returned the smile and leaned over, poised to plant a kiss on her lips. At the last moment she turned her face so his lips found her cheek instead. He drew back with a look of surprise. Lucy hurried into the house before he could say anything. She banged the door shut even though she heard him calling for her.

"What's going on, Lucy? And what happened to your overalls?"

Lucy looked over at Momma, who stood holding a mixing

bowl against her frilled apron.

"I slipped in the river, but I'm fine."

"Oh, Lucy. I don't know why you insist on traipsing around like you were some man."

"We saw some soldiers today," she said hastily, hoping to change the subject.

"Yes, I heard some neighboring boys just joined up. Did you know your classmate, Henry Glass, is one of them? I must say I'm thankful Carl and Tim are too young. Can you imagine waiting to hear when they might have to go over and face those terrible Japanese or the Germans? I couldn't bear the thought of it. I'd worry day and night. I don't know how others do it."

"No, I mean we saw soldiers *here*. They're going to train on Seneca Rocks. They're planning to make camp right on the Hoppers' field. We met a couple of them today while Allen and I were at the river."

Momma set down her bowl and glanced out between the parted cotton curtains. "Oh dear, I wish they didn't have to come here. Not that I'm against our fighting men, but things are so difficult with the war right now." She stared a bit longer. "Lucy, why is Allen sitting on our front porch? Did you leave him there without inviting him in?"

Lucy felt the warmth rush into her cheeks. She looked out the window and saw Allen sitting on the steps, a pencil and slip of paper in his hand, writing a note.

"Go see if he would like a glass of lemonade."

Lucy knew what he really wanted, but she wasn't about to let him kiss her for real. Nor did she know when she would ever be ready for that. At least not with Allen. "It's all right, Momma. I—I think it would be better for me not to talk to him right now."

Momma gave her a quizzical look. "Now what? Don't tell me you two had an argument."

"No. I need to change out of these wet overalls. Excuse me." Lucy headed for the stairs and her room, thankful to have escaped another encounter with Allen on the front porch. She just couldn't imagine being kissed on the lips by the man. He was a childhood friend, after all. A buddy. Not the man she should kiss and then marry. She flopped down on the bed and stared up at the ceiling. Instead of Allen, she suddenly envisioned the handsome army captain named Nick Landers coming toward her with a bunch of flowers in his hand. He would give them to her, accompanied by his ever-ready smile and a hearty laugh that tickled her insides. His tall frame would tower over her. And then he would stoop and ever so slowly, with great emotion, kiss her full on the lips.

"Lucy, Allen is downstairs!" Momma called up.

She sighed and tossed a bed pillow. *Oh please, not now.* "I have a headache!" she called back. It was true. Already she felt the tension creeping up her neck and into the back of her head from her emotional turmoil. After a few anxious minutes, she heard the front door shut, then footsteps on the stairs. The door to her room opened a crack.

"Really, Lucy," Momma admonished, handing her a note. "I don't know what's gotten into you. Do you really have a headache or is something else bothering you?"

"I don't know, Momma. Thank you for bringing me the note."

Momma gave her one last look before heading down the stairs. Lucy unfolded the paper and read Allen's message—

which included many misspellings. It said he would be in Elkins for a week and when he returned, to be ready for a wonderful night out to finish what they had started today. She refolded the note and set it on the lamp table. *What is it we're supposed to finish, Allen?* she thought. *Have we really started anything? I mean, I like you and all. We've been friends since we learned to talk. But are we really supposed to be together? Am I supposed to be your girl? Even marry you? Or should we just stay friends?*

Lucy began to shiver again like she had back at the river. Only then did she realize she was still wearing her wet overalls. When she stood up, a damp impression remained on the bedspread. *Now I am losing my mind. But why? Can it all be because of those soldiers we met in the fields today, and especially one named Captain Nick Landers?*

two

Nick Landers loosened his laces and yanked off the stiff boots, thankful for the cool air that refreshed his aching toes. He should be used to this military show by now, but every day yielded surprises in one form or another. And after today's encounter in the fields, he sensed his time here at Seneca Rocks would be no different.

Nick glanced up and squinted. From where Fred had hastily erected their tent for the evening, he could see the darkened scales of rock jutting toward the sky. They weren't much compared to the mountain terrain where he grew up and where he'd trained—the Rocky Mountains of Colorado, which had year-round snow at the uppermost peaks. He loved those mountains. On such peaks, adventure loomed all year. Skiing, climbing, camping—all the things he loved to do and had perfected with time. When he heard from his ski instructor that the army was looking for men to help train outdoor and survival techniques to enlisted men, Nick knew he had the skill to do it. But he hadn't imagined it would lead him here, to the backwoods of West Virginia where vertical sheets of rock would become a training ground for numerous soldiers before they left for Europe.

But he didn't have anything drawing his heart back to Colorado. There was no woman waiting for him. Donna had been jealous of the mountains and the way they affected him, the mountains she insisted stole Nick from her.

"You keep skiing and climbing like this and we'll have to say our good-byes," Donna once threatened. He never took her seriously, until that day at the soda fountain. They were supposed to be sipping ice-cream floats and having a nice conversation about the future. Instead, she turned the meeting into a Dear John encounter, minus the letter. Nick never saw it coming, though thinking back on it, he should have. Donna had dropped enough hints. Yet when she told him they were through, he balked.

"I don't understand. I thought you liked what I do. You never said anything otherwise."

"You never have enough time for me, Nick," she complained. "And if you remember anything at all, I did say plenty about it. You just never stopped to listen."

"I asked you to come out and see what I do."

"Like your mountaineering is some baseball game, and I'm supposed to be the lovesick girl swooning in the stands," she grumbled. "Don't you understand that girls want to feel special? That we don't want to feel like we have to chase you men around all the time, especially not up some mountain? That sometimes we want to be the ones chased?"

Nick remembered the ice cream melting into his soda until it had turned into a white, frothy film floating on top. Never had he imagined Donna was so unhappy. She'd always had a smile on her face for him—or so it appeared. She talked about everything happening in her life. They went to dances. They would take walks in the woods. Did she really have that much discontent in her, simmering like some pot of stew, ready to boil over at the least provocation? Or maybe it was something else altogether. Like another man.

When he broached the subject, she turned as red as an apple.

Her hand clenched her purse, as if she might clobber him with it. She rose from the counter in a fury. "How dare you even say that, Nicholas Landers! As if you think you're some king of the mountain. Let me tell you, you're no king. You–you're a—a—regular nincompoop!" With that she stalked out of the shop.

He saw her once after that, on a street corner, before he left for Camp Hale. She looked at him, a stony expression on her face. He could tell right away things had irrevocably collapsed between them. She then spun about on one high heel and disappeared.

And that was that.

For a while he thought about her words, pondering whether the mountains had become some obsession in his life, keeping him away from her and life in general. Soon after that he'd had little time to ponder its significance. He poured all his energy into readying himself and the men from Camp Hale to head east, to this area where he would be teaching them rock climbing techniques. Now he had one job and one job alone: to train the men to climb Seneca Rocks with courage and ease.

Nick had never been east of the Mississippi before coming to West Virginia. Denver had always been his home. His family still lived there. When he first arrived here, he marveled at how small the Appalachian Mountains were. And they were thick with vegetation. Trees lined the very summits, unlike the bare peaks above the tree line of the Rockies.

Then today, he'd had his first encounter with the natives. West Virginian folk like the young woman he saw by the river, clad in wet overalls, holding on to the arm of a freckle-faced, red-haired young man who looked like he might have been running a lemonade stand. Nick had casually glanced at the materials that had been given to him—a book on mountain lore, describing the people who lived here. It was as if the higher-ups were readying them for entering another culture, even though they were still in the United States. But the people weren't backward, not by any means. He'd found the young woman in her wet overalls to be the adventurous type, even if she was uncertain about their presence. And she hadn't complained once about her damp clothing. As far as he knew, Donna had never worn a pair of pants in her life, let alone overalls soaked in a mountain river. But this woman wore them all right, hitched up enough to expose a portion of her calves. Most of all she had spunk. He liked the picture.

"I said, have you finished looking over our supply list?" a voice spoke loudly in his ear.

Nick jumped and turned, only to see his friend Fred staring at him with a funny smirk on his face. "Actually, no."

"I could tell. You'd better come down off your mountaintop there, Captain, and back to solid ground. And we haven't even started climbing and rappelling yet."

"I was thinking about those people we met by the river earlier today."

Fred hooted. "They didn't look too eager to make anyone's acquaintance. Especially ours."

"Yes, but they live in this area. They know it well and probably know the terrain like the backs of their hands. Maybe we should try to find them. We could use a guide or two to show us where to access the rocks. Scouting out all the trails and such will take a lot of time. And maybe we can make some friends with the locals."

"Are you joking? We need to do it ourselves. Like I said, that fellow there looked about ready to spit nails. The dame was kind of cute, I'll have to admit, even if she was dressed in overalls. A perfect picture of country living, the two of them, don't you think?"

"I think we just startled them is all. I mean, how would you like it if you were by the river, having a grand old time, maybe even ready for a kiss, then suddenly a huge army truck comes barreling down at you?"

"I'd have jumped out of the way and offered a salute."

Nick slapped his friend on the shoulder. "Sure you would. Since when do rules and regulations mean that much to you?"

"What? They mean plenty to me. We'd have no army without them. And if we're going to defeat the enemy, we'd better make sure we're following the rules."

"Good point. As it is, you and I have been a little lax about fraternization. We'll have to be more careful about that," Nick said thoughtfully, then smiled. "So here's a direct order from your commanding officer: We will go track down that young couple to find out more about this area, Sergeant Watkins. And make new friends, too."

"Friends, sure," he murmured.

"I'd like to hear you say, 'Yes, sir. On the double, sir.'"

"I lost that with you long ago, don't you remember?" he said with a grin. "Hey, I may still be heading up raw recruits, trying to get them ready to scale rocks as thin as gingersnaps. But as far as the 'sir' routine with you, I thought we'd dealt with that. Like on that icy cliff back in Colorado when I saved you, and you said rank didn't matter." He paused. "But it was a while ago, I suppose. I'll offer a salute if that will help."

Nick shook his head, though he couldn't help the slight smile creasing his face. How typical of Fred's personality. "So, getting back to my original order—can I count on you,

Sergeant Watkins, to help me find the guides we need?"

Fred righted himself and offered a salute, accompanied by a mischievous smile.

Nick waved him on. "Let's get going then. That fellow said his father owned the only store around here. I'm sure we can find it."

"Sure, I'll come along, Captain. There isn't much around here to keep me busy. It will be a few days before the boys arrive."

Nick reached for his boots and jammed them back onto his feet, ignoring the pain of having his toes crammed once more into a tight space with no room to spare. He and Fred then started across the tall fields of grass, inhaling the fresh air. What a pleasant place this was, even if it was West Virginia. No, the mountains weren't like the Rockies, but they were mountains in their own right and quite beautiful. Especially the site where they would be training—nearly nine hundred vertical feet of jagged stone.

Looking back at the face of Seneca Rocks, Nick felt a sudden desire to head over there with his gear and begin climbing. He could tell Fred they needed to try out some climbing routes before the troops arrived.

Nick refused to think about what might happen to them once their training was complete. For all he knew, they could be shipped to Europe, perhaps never to return. He held the idea of that possibility down in a deep reservoir inside himself, along with his fear of the unknown. He would take it one day at a time. And right now, his job was seeking out the young woman in the overalls—and perhaps her ill-mannered boyfriend—to find out more about the rocks he planned to scale with his trainees.

As Nick and Fred walked along the main road, they received many stares from people in the automobiles that passed them by. One gray-haired woman tugged on her elderly husband's arm and pointed. "Look at the soldiers, Barnaby!" she exclaimed.

"We seem to be causing quite a stir with the local folks," Fred mused. "Like they don't know there's a war going on."

"Maybe they don't. This isn't Main Street, America. Look where they live, out in the middle of nowhere. They probably lead sheltered lives. I don't even know if there's a theater around here. And who knows if they get any of the radio broadcasts."

"Well, if they don't know about the war by now, then they really are living in a hole in the ground. Everyone's heard about Pearl Harbor."

Just then another automobile drove by. The horn honked, and the driver waved.

"See?" Nick pointed out. "There's some support to be had around here. Someone knows about us."

"It's probably the general, arriving incognito for a surprise inspection," Fred added.

Nick snickered. Soon they came to a fork in the road with a store sitting at the junction.

"There it is. Hopper General Store. That was easy." He inhaled a breath. "Now comes the hard part." He headed toward the establishment with Fred following close behind. Several young men standing on the front porch ceased their chatter and stared. A little girl ran to her daddy, pointing back at the soldiers. Nick felt as if he were an invader on these people's land rather than a defender of freedom. When they entered the store, an older woman was standing at the counter with several items. She turned and gasped at the sight of Nick towering over her. "Land sakes, what are you men doing here? Are the Japanese coming here?"

"No, ma'am. We're just here to do some training on the rocks."

"Whatever for?"

"Well, there are lots of rocks and cliffs over in Europe. So we're going to train our soldiers how to climb them so they'll be ready to drive away the enemy when the orders are given."

She blinked, looking as if she didn't quite comprehend what he was saying before finishing her purchase.

"I need your coupon for the sugar, Matilda," said the man behind the counter.

She opened her pocketbook and fumbled through its contents. "Oh, dear. I must have left it at home. I'll bring it tomorrow."

The man looked at her and then at Nick and Fred. "Sorry, Matilda. Got to have it. We have military men among us. Need to go by the rules or it looks bad."

Fred laughed. "If I wanted to go into police work, I sure wouldn't be here." He paused. "Not to say this isn't a nice place, even if it is located in the middle of nowhere."

"We're pretty proud of our home," the man said, offering his hand. "Ed Hopper. I heard you boys were coming. Saw the announcement."

Nick breathed a sigh of relief. "That's good to know word got around. From what your son said, he didn't seem to know anything about it."

"Well, folks might know but sometimes it doesn't sink in. They kind of lead their own lives here, you see. So you met Allen?"

"By the river earlier today. He didn't seem too happy that we were on your land."

Ed Hopper waved his hand. He then shoved the sugar, canned meat, and other staples into a paper bag. "Bring that coupon tomorrow, Matilda, all right?"

"Thank you kindly," she said, sidestepping away from Nick and Fred.

"Allen doesn't know a good deal about what's happening," the father continued. "He's got his mind set on one thing. His girl. That's all he thinks about."

"Sure, that happens to many young fellows in love," Fred mused. "The captain here knows all about that. His girl didn't appreciate his first love. Mountain climbing, that is."

Ed smiled. "Around here we all like the mountains. They're a part of life. And I hope they do well for you."

Nick began to relax. At last God had led them to someone who not only understood the importance of why the soldiers were here but was giving them encouragement.

Suddenly Ed Hopper stepped out from behind the counter and fetched two cold sodas from a large red case. "Welcome to Seneca Rocks."

"Thank you, sir!" Fred said with enthusiasm, using the bottle opener mounted on the side of the counter, then taking a long swig. "That hits the spot."

"Mr. Hopper, we need assistance from someone who knows the rocks," Nick said. "Someone who could show us around, perhaps? I was hoping maybe your son and even his girl could help us out. They looked like they know this place pretty well."

"Well, Allen just left to run some errands for me in Elkins, and he'll be gone all week. Lucy knows the land around here. Lived here all her life, just like many of us. But I'm not sure her folks would take kindly to her traipsing off with military fellars all by herself."

"Certainly not, and I wouldn't want her to. What about her father? Could he be of help?"

"Sure. Dick Bland would help you out if he's not busy at the mill. They live up the road there, about a half mile. White house with a front porch. Can't miss it."

"Thank you. And thanks for the soda."

Ed nodded, turning his attention to another customer who had ventured forward to make a purchase. Nick and Fred wandered up the road. By the time the house materialized in the distance, the sun had begun its departure behind the ridge of mountains. Evening shadows seeped across the land. "We may need to continue this another time," Fred commented. "It'll be dark soon."

"We can at least introduce ourselves and see if anyone is willing to help." Nick slowly mounted the porch steps. A dog bounded out from behind the house and latched on to Nick's pant leg. "Hey!" he shouted at the snarling canine. "Ouch! Let go!"

Faces peered out from behind the parted curtains. He could hear the voices of boys calling for their mother. The door opened a crack and a woman peered out. "Can I help you?"

"Sorry to disturb you, ma'am," Fred began, removing his cap while Nick continued trying to shake his leg free from the dog's toothy grip.

"Carl, Jeepers got off his rope again!" the woman yelled. "Come tie him up!"

"Jeepers knows better than that," another female voice said as a young woman stepped out from behind the woman. She stopped short and stared. "You again! What are you doing here?"

"Lucy, you know these men?" the woman asked.

"No, Momma. Well, in a way. Allen and I—we—we saw them by the river earlier today." She lowered her head and stared down at her feet as if embarrassed to reveal the fact. Her damp overalls had been replaced by a fresh pair. Her hands now slid into the front pockets of her new overalls, where they remained.

"Do you need something?" the mother now directed to Nick and Fred as Lucy brushed by them to retrieve the dog. Nick couldn't help watching Lucy interact with the dog, speaking kindly to it, scratching the pooch around the ears as she led the dog away. Meanwhile Fred tried to explain their need for a guide.

"I think you've come to the wrong place," the woman said. "We don't climb those rocks."

"I know about the rocks, Momma!" piped up a young boy.

"That's enough, Tim. It's getting dark and soon it will be time for bed."

"Momma!" he protested.

At this point, Fred yanked on Nick's sleeve and shook his head. "I think this is a dead end," he whispered, retreating off the porch stairs. "Sorry to have bothered you, ma'am. We'll ask around maybe in the morning."

She nodded and closed the door. The men turned to leave but not before Nick spied Lucy standing nearby, having completed her duty with the dog. "Sorry we startled you out there in the field today," he said. "I hope you didn't get hurt in the river."

"I didn't. Allen was the one who caused me to fall in the river."

Nick hesitated. "You go there a lot?"

She laughed. "All the time. I live here, you know. And our cattle graze right next to the Hoppers' land."

"Ever been up to the rocks?"

"Of course. They're wonderful. It's like a different world up there."

"Maybe you know someone who could help us look around for trails and climbing routes to the top?" he asked hopefully.

She shook her head. "I've never climbed them. They're too dangerous. You could fall off."

"Not with the right equipment. You'd be surprised what you can do these days." Nick felt Fred nudge him again. "Well, if you think of someone who could help us out, let me know. We're down at the camp in the field." Nick wheeled and headed for the road.

Soon the sound of Fred's silly singsong interrupted the quiet evening. "Do you know the rocks here, m'dear, oh m'dear? Do you know them? Do you know the river clear, m'dear, oh m'dear? Do you know them?"

"What are you doing?"

"I'm singing a ballad about an elite mountain climber and a mountain dame from the wilds of West Virginia, Captain."

"You've got some strange ideas roaming about in your mind, friend. I was trying to find someone who could help us."

"Of course, sir. I don't suppose we'll mention some of the other things you were trying to find out, too."

"You're right, we won't, because there wasn't anything. Besides, she has a boyfriend already. You saw him."

"Of course. Whatever you say."

Nick said no more, hoping Fred would likewise forget the whole thing. But he had to admit he liked the idea of knowing a young woman who enjoyed the mountains as much as he did. Donna had never set one foot on them. Lucy, as her mother called her, seemed to breathe them. Just as he did. He shook his head. There was no sense pondering it. They were only here a few weeks and then he would be gone. Where to, he didn't know. But there certainly was no time to think of another woman, not after his experience with Donna. Even if this Lucy loved the mountains. . .just like he did.

three

"Of course I would love to show you the rocks, Captain Landers. What? Alone? Well, it's not like we're really alone now, are we? God is watching over us. And I know we can find what you need to know, sure enough." Lucy then grinned her fullest, her teeth gleaming back from her reflection in the mirror. Her hand slid through the length of her bobbed brown hair. She smiled again, turned to one side, and smiled once more. *This is no good. I can't stand here pretending to have a man fall in love with me, dressed in overalls.* She went over to the wardrobe and pulled out a cotton dress. After taking off her blouse and overalls, she slipped the dress up and over her head and then returned to the mirror, grinning broadly at her beaming reflection. She took the folds of the dress in her hands and spun around. "Oh, this old thing? Well, thank you, Captain Landers. It's so nice of you to say so."

"Hee hee hee."

"Ah ha ha ha!"

Lucy whirled to find thirteen-year-old Carl and eleven-year-old Tim peeking around the door. "How dare you!" she shouted at them, throwing open the door. They scattered like squirrels, racing for the stairs.

"Can't catch us!" Tim shouted in glee.

"I don't plan to catch you. I have better things to do with my time."

"Yeah, like pretending that soldier is your sweetheart or

something," Carl sneered. Then in a high, squeaky voice, his fist planted against his cheek, he continued. "Oh, honey, sure I'll take you to the rocks. Whatever your little ol' heart wants! In fact, let's just pucker up while we're at it!" He laughed. "Bet Allen gets real mad when he finds out."

"Why, you little snitch. Don't you dare say anything to Allen. And I—I don't even know the soldier anyway. I'm just having some fun." She shut the door, then turned back, staring at the mirror once more and the dress that hung on her thin form. Angry tears burned her eyes. She took off the dress, wondering what in the world had possessed her to put it on, knowing her two nosy brothers were always spying on her. Lucy hung the dress carefully in the wardrobe.

What was she doing, fantasizing about a military man like Nick Landers? She paused to think about that one. Like she told her brothers, she didn't know the first thing about the man, except that he was here to climb her beloved rocks.

On the other hand, she did know Allen inside and out—everything about him, it seemed. His likes and dislikes. His emotions. His internal battles that sometimes raged more than she cared to see. But to her, Allen was a friend. A childhood playmate. Someone she had grown up with. Not a hero by any means, though he had offered to give her his shirt after she had fallen into the river—not that the shirt would have made her feel any drier.

Allen had always been around. He'd once brought lilies from his mother's garden when Lucy was sick. He was always able to obtain supplies from the store for her family if ever the need arose. And she had agreed on a date at the soda fountain with him when he returned from Elkins, to go over some important news.

Lucy began to tremble. What if that important news signaled his desire for a deeper commitment between them—like marriage? "How can I marry Allen?" she said aloud. She couldn't even picture him as a father, taking up the reins of the family as the head of the house with her by his side. The picture she saw instead was the two of them sharing an ice-cream cone while climbing up to the viewpoint just below the rocky summit, chatting about the neighbors or sharing some memory from grade school.

Lucy put on her blouse and overalls once more. Slowly she went downstairs to find the house was empty. Everyone had disappeared. Momma had gone to help sew a quilt with the elderly Mrs. Sampson. The boys probably went next door to play with the neighbor's children. Daddy had left at dawn to work at the lumber mill. She was all alone.

Stepping outside, the bright sunshine greeted her from another pleasant summer day. Nearby in the corral, a horse nickered at her. A fine day for a ride. Maybe she could head toward Seneca Rocks, just to see what might be happening with the soldiers who had been arriving this past week. She had seen many trucks rumbling along the road, bringing men and equipment to the valley. "How about a ride, Maple Sugar?" she asked the tan-colored mare. The horse bobbed its head as if nodding in agreement. Lucy saddled the horse, one of two their family owned. Later that evening the boys would go round up the few head of cattle Daddy still owned. Momma often asked him when he was going to sell them. But with the onset of war, he'd decided to hold on to them as their bread and butter should things go awry.

Lucy rode Maple Sugar down the road, waved at the driver of an automobile who honked a friendly greeting her way.

She passed the Hoppers' store, where the usual neighbors gathered on the porch to swap tales. Then she caught sight of the mountains, looming above her in all their grandeur, just as she'd seen them all her life. Seneca Rocks. What a spectacle to behold, and one that still caused her to draw a breath of awe. A natural wonder chiseled by the hand of God. She couldn't fathom how the touch of His hand had made these rocks jut into the air. Nor could she comprehend how men like Nick Landers could go way up there and climb the rocky faces. The closest she had been to them was a point near the rocks where the forest opened to reveal a spectacular view. She was too scared to venture any farther. Now she couldn't help but marvel at Nick's bravery.

The thought of him made her guide the horse down the road. When Lucy reached the fields, she observed the array of green tents standing in rows, one after the other, as if the tents themselves were part of some vast company ready for inspection. The sight proved strange on a field normally occupied by cattle and horses. For now, the animals had been moved to a separate part of the pasture, behind a row of fencing. She wondered what Allen would think of this massive intrusion on the family land when he returned from Elkins.

Lucy dismounted and tied up the horse, ready to investigate the sight. Men moved about in groups, appearing like ants, hard at work at various tasks. About twenty of them were constructing a strange wooden contraption, the likes of which she had never seen. It looked to her like some gigantic beehive. *What could that be?*

Curiosity got the better of her. Momma often scolded Lucy for the way she snooped around, saying she was always far too interested in what was happening. Today was no different.

Lucy simply had to know what they were building and why.

Approaching the outskirts of the camp on foot, Lucy was suddenly stopped by two guards. Their helmets boasted the large white letters *MP*. "Sorry, miss, but you can't come through here. This area is off-limits to civilians."

"But my friend owns this land," she said. "In fact, our cattle are grazing right over there. It's the Hopper family's."

"Sorry. It's the rules."

"Would it help if I said that Captain Nick Landers asked me to come?"

The two guards looked at each other. "You have proof of that?"

"He came just the other day to my house. He and some other man. They were looking for someone to guide them to Seneca Rocks where he's gonna be climbing. He told me all about it." She placed her hands on her hips. "If you don't believe me, go ask him yourself. Tell him Lucy Bland has come with information about the rocks."

The guards conversed with each other. Finally, one of them headed off in the direction of the wooden beehive. Lucy could see men exchanging words. One of the men stepped away from the group and straightened, as if straining to see in her direction. The man, dressed in a gray T-shirt and green pants, lumbered over, accompanied by the guard.

"Miss Bland, what are you doing here?"

Nick Landers looked even better than what she'd imagined that morning in front of the mirror. The T-shirt he wore displayed his strong muscles. Sweat glistened on his limbs and face. How she wished she were wearing that pretty dress instead of dingy overalls that made her feel unkempt and immature.

"Hello, Captain Landers. You said if I knew of someone who could guide you to Seneca Rocks that I was to find you."

"She's all right," he informed the guards. "Thank you." They saluted and moved off. "Okay, so who did you find?"

Lucy couldn't help grinning. She slid her hands into the pockets of her overalls. "Why, me, of course."

"You."

"Certainly. Who else?"

He scratched the top of his head. "I'm sorry, Miss Bland, but I don't think it would be proper for a fine young woman like you to take a bunch of gritty soldiers on a grand tour of the rocks. Not that I doubt your knowledge or experience. I was hoping maybe you had talked to your daddy or someone else about doing it. Or maybe an uncle or a friend. Even that fellow who was with you."

"Allen would sooner show you a copperhead, I think. We have a lot of them around here, you know. Good thing you all wear those boots. You never know when you might stumble onto one of them."

"I'll have to remember that, thank you. I guess you'd better not ask him then. Sure don't want anymore hard feelings."

"He's gone to Elkins. Hey, what is that thing they're building?"

"What?" He followed her finger as she pointed out the large beehive in the distance. "Oh. You mean the corncrib."

Lucy laughed long and loud, which spawned a smile on his face. "That is no corncrib, Captain Landers. I ought to know what a corncrib looks like. That looks more like a huge wooden beehive. Or tower of some sort."

"I've never heard it called a beehive. That's a new one." He began to walk toward it.

Lucy followed eagerly, past some tents and a few soldiers milling about. They all stared at her. Some smiled. Others looked inquisitive, as if wondering why one of their training leaders was conversing with the likes of her. It felt strange to be walking through a military camp. Lucy had seen pictures of such things, of course. Now with soldiers and their equipment nearly in her own backyard, she felt as if the war had become very personal. In a way it left her anxious. With Nick by her side, though, she felt strangely protected, as if he might give his life for her if the enemy were to invade. She liked the feeling. Not that Allen didn't protect her at times or show his concern. But there were things about Nick that were different. His strength of purpose. His determination. He wasn't a friendly soul like Allen but someone completely different. And maybe by spending this time with him, she would find out exactly who he was.

"This is our corncrib, beehive, tower, or whatever you want to call it," he said rather proudly as he gestured to the officer supervising the construction.

The officer nodded, issued an order to his men, and the group moved away.

Lucy studied the contraption made of wood. "I'm afraid to ask what you might be doing with this, Captain Landers. Dare I?"

He smiled. "Dare away. We'll soon have plenty of green recruits who have never even used climbing gear, much less climb rocks like you have here. So we plan to have the boys first climb the wooden tower to give them a feel for the ropes and the techniques involved in rock climbing. They'll learn how to climb and rappel while becoming familiar with the commands we use. Climbers need to understand all the technical aspects before making an actual climb along a marked pitch. That's a steep portion of a vertical rock that requires the use of ropes for safety. Or belaying, where a climber protects a fellow climber as he ascends by holding a safety rope."

Lucy listened intently. "I wouldn't need any fancy climbing gear to climb a tower like that," she said. Impulsively, she brushed by him, placing one foot on the wooden slats of the structure to begin hoisting herself up.

"Miss Bland, please don't go any farther," he said as he reached out to her. "I'm sure you can climb this without being roped in, but I don't want anything to happen to you. As it is, it's still not completed. Please come down."

Just hearing him speak such words of concern sent Lucy stepping back down off the wooden contraption, directly into Nick Landers's arms. She inhaled a breath, trying to steady the rapid beating of her heart.

Almost as quickly he stepped back, adjusting the cap he wore. "I guess that's enough excitement for one day," he said rather sheepishly. He glanced over at several men standing in the distance, observing them with interest.

At that moment a whistle pierced the air. "Fred," he muttered.

"What was that, Captain Landers?"

He shook his head. "Nothing, nothing at all, Miss Bland."

"Could you just call me Lucy? The last time I was called Miss Bland was by my sixth grade teacher who didn't like the way I wrote my paper on what I want to do when I grow up."

"What did you write about?"

His question caught her off guard. No one ever asked what she wanted to do with her life. At that moment she didn't know, either, except to go with Nick up to the rocks. "I'm not sure what I wrote. It was a long time ago. I guess what every girl wants. Be a wife and mother. Maybe a teacher or a nurse. That kind of thing. By the way, can I call you Nick?"

"Well, uh. . ." He glanced toward the men, including the one who had visited her house with Nick. They began to disperse under his glaring eye to engage in other duties. "I suppose while I'm here in camp, my title would be best. You see, I need the men to respect me, and using my rank helps accomplish that. It's a matter of military protocol."

"Of course," Lucy purred.

A bit of red filled in the tips of his ears, as if the familiarity of being on a first-name basis somehow made him shy. But Nick Landers was far from being shy when it came to life. His life seemed filled with adventure. What must he have experienced that brought him to this place and time, to begin training soldiers on Seneca Rocks? How she would love to know more about him. She didn't want to intrude on his privacy, yet she found him fascinating enough to want to know everything. "So what did you want to do back when you were in sixth grade?"

"What I'm doing right now. That is, anything to do with the mountains. Hiking them. Climbing them. Skiing them."

"People do those things here. I've never even been on a pair of skis. But I do like to climb mountains, using the trails, of course. That's why I thought I could help you and your men at Seneca Rocks. I know the area really well."

He smiled once more. "Lucy, I appreciate the offer, but again, I think it might be better if we find a man to help out. Not that you couldn't do it, I know," he added hastily. "I just don't want your father or that young man of yours coming after me with a shotgun because you're leading a bunch of rough military men up the side of a mountain."

Lucy giggled. "It's not like I haven't gone up the mountain with a man before." Now it was her turn to feel the warmth in her face and running down her neck. "What I meant to say is, Allen and I have gone up there near the summit of the rocks plenty of times."

"You mean you've gone up there with your boyfriend?"

"He's not my boyfriend. Not really, though he might think he is. We're just friends. We've known each other since we were born, practically." She shuffled her feet, her gaze taking in the rows of green tents before her. "So where do you stay? I hope not in one of those tiny tents."

"We have an officers' tent, one of the bigger ones. But I've stayed in small tents. Even went without a tent once, in a blizzard, of all things."

Lucy stared. "How did you keep from freezing?"

"Snow is actually quite an effective insulator. It kept me pretty warm. You can make a shelter of sorts with it. That's part of the survival techniques one should learn before going into the mountains."

Lucy considered the idea of camping in a tent made of snow and trembled at the thought. "I'm sorry, but a snow tent is not my idea of a fine shelter. I'd need a solid roof over my head in a storm like that. We get some good snows here. The mountains are very pretty with snow on them, especially Seneca Rocks. They look like upside-down icicles."

For a moment neither of them said anything. Nick's gaze wandered from her to the tent city and back again, as if he were preoccupied by something. How she wished she knew what he was thinking. Maybe one day those deep thoughts he had would become audible. At least he didn't seem to mind conversing with a girl dressed in overalls, although she would have preferred to be wearing a dress right now. Maybe one day she and Nick could make their escape to the viewpoint just below the rocky summit with a picnic lunch and take in the scenery together.

The man Nick called Fred came up then, tentatively at first, to show Nick some paperwork he had hidden behind his back. "You remember Fred—er, Sergeant Watkins, don't you, Lucy?" Nick asked.

"Yes. How are you?"

"Oh, just fine, miss." Then turning to Nick he said, "Excuse me for interrupting, Captain, but I have some things here I need to go over with you."

"I need to get going, Lucy. Duty calls."

"Of course. Thank you for showing me your, uh, corncrib–beehive contraption, Captain Landers. If you need anything now, just let me know. Anything at all. We all want to make you feel at home."

"Thanks. I appreciate it."

Lucy wandered off, looking over her shoulder at the men now jabbering away, about what she couldn't tell. Her feet were slow to return to where she had left Maple Sugar tied to a fence post. All good things must come to an end, though she wished they wouldn't. But she knew Nick was here for one duty and one duty only. It wasn't to make eyes at her. Or ask her out on a date. Or become her man. He was here to train his men. But things could change. Maybe after this meeting, Nick would feel differently about her. There were other mountains to conquer besides those he could see with his eyes. She would be most willing to have him climb the mountain of love with her if the opportunity arose.

four

"Whoever thought you would go for some mountain dame from the wilds of West Virginia? Then again, when you think about it, it makes complete sense. The mountains are your life. Why not have a wife from the mountains? It would be the perfect complement, like gravy with mashed potatoes."

Nick tried to ignore the gibes of his friend and concentrate on the tasks before him. Instead, Fred took every opportunity to make remarks about Lucy's impromptu visit. In Nick's eyes, Lucy was a young lady looking to make a friendly impression on the soldiers who had come to her valley. And yes, her visit had made an impression on him, though he would never let Fred know. "She was just being friendly. Let it go."

"Well, it looks to me like she considers a certain climbing captain more than just a friend," Fred continued. "You could see it. When she came here, you should have told her to leave, that you were too busy. Instead you gave her the grand tour and then some. An interesting way to feed an appetite, don't you think?"

"You must be missing Alice," Nick retorted, thrusting the paperwork into Fred's hands. "It's the only reason I can think of for this continued pestering of your CO. Unless there's some jealousy mixed in there, too?"

"Have you forgotten that I know you? That we went through blizzards and rocks in Colorado? That I saved your neck more than once, my friend, if you remember?"

"That's why I make certain you're on the other end of the climbing rope, Fred. You've never let go, even when you've been tempted to, no doubt. So when's the last time you heard from Alice?"

Fred shook his head and strode off, muttering to himself. Nick knew he'd hit a sore spot by mentioning Fred's girl. For several weeks now, Fred had worried that Alice was about to send him a Dear John letter. Many of the men had received them or been dumped like Nick had when Donna discarded him like an empty milk bottle on the doorstep, all on account of his interest in mountain adventures. He rubbed his chin, thinking of Lucy's eagerness to show him anything having to do with the mountains.

What a difference between Lucy and Donna. Like night and day. Donna had become like a storm cloud. For certain, Lucy was like sunshine and he'd come all this way, to a beautiful place in the middle of nowhere in the wilds of West Virginia, before finally meeting her. If only he had met Lucy in Colorado, instead of Donna. Sadly, he would only be here for a few weeks and then the training would end. From there, he couldn't begin to fathom what might happen or where he might end up.

Nick pushed the thoughts aside when a line of soldiers marched up—the first of the raw recruits they would begin training in rock climbing techniques. With their youthful faces, they looked like schoolboys to Nick. They seemed fearful and anxious. All of them were probably wondering what they would be doing in the days ahead.

Several of the privates offered meager salutes to Nick. Fred began barking at them to stand at attention. "At ease," Nick said with an elbow toward Fred.

"Sir, excuse me, sir, but are we gonna climb that?" a baby-faced soldier inquired in a tremulous voice, pointing to the distant rocks.

"You certainly are, Private."

All of the recruits stared in shock and dismay. Some shook their heads. Assorted whispers filled the air. "No way can I do that." "Are they crazy?" "They can't make me do that. Fighting the enemy is bad enough."

"You'll do all of it and more. Sergeant Watkins and I are going to be there to guide you every step of the way."

"Excuse me, sir, but I was scared to even climb the loft in our barn."

Nick wanted to encourage the men with a verse that helped him when his courage waned. He straightened and placed his hands behind his back. "Men, I've done a lot of work on the rocks. I've been in snows higher than your heads. Through it all, I've come to believe in the protection of a mighty God over my life. I know He is with me. And I believe I can do all things through Him who gives me strength. Make that your motto in life, and you will surely succeed in everything you put your mind to. Like climbing these rocks."

Nick didn't know if the words affected the men, but he found strength just by speaking the verse. He indeed wanted to do all things but only through Him who imparted the strength he needed, even when the going got difficult. Like when he was lost, frozen, and nearly found his toes sacrificed to frostbite. Or had men freeze on the rocks or go off trail. And for himself, when love began to wane and he wondered what the future held, especially with the tide of war and not knowing how they would all be involved in this affair, the strength of that scripture sustained him.

"Now that that's taken care of, let's get you assigned," Fred said, giving Nick a sideways glance. Nick knew his friend disliked anything with a religious connotation to it. Much like his remarks about Lucy, Fred had often ribbed Nick about his faith. How could God let the Japanese bomb Pearl Harbor and kill so many sailors? Or let the Germans overrun countries and hurt innocent people like the Jews? At times Nick felt confused by these events, too. But he could not relinquish his faith, especially when it came to matters he did not understand. God had His purposes. As simple human beings, they could never understand the whole picture. Maybe Nick wouldn't understand this either until they were in Europe, driving away the enemy, liberating besieged towns. Maybe then he would understand it all.

Nick felt a new determination surge through him then, determination to conquer the rocks here and then the rocks in Italy or wherever the high command sent them. He would help the men overcome their doubts and fears. He would teach them how to rise to the occasion and overcome the mountains, both within and without. And they would march forth, proclaiming victory, setting the captives free.

When Fred returned from assigning the men to their respective companies, he plunked himself down. Nick had spread out a topography map before him to study the terrain. "So what was all that about?" Fred asked.

"What?"

"That display of religiosity before the men. C'mon, Nick."

"Captain Landers, Sergeant."

Fred threw up his hands.

Nick set down his pencil where he had been taking notes. "Look, I saw the fear in those young men's eyes. We need to come across as confident leaders if we want them to do things that maybe none of them have ever done before. And I know that without God, I couldn't begin to do the things I'm called to do."

"I'm just asking why you have to bring God into everything, Captain, *sir*. I thought we would keep religion separate from our duties here."

"Anyone who separates duty from God is foolish. Without God there is no sense of duty. You were the one commenting on the need for rules and regulations so we can defeat the enemy. If you can't believe and devote your life to a higher being, then why have rules in the first place? Why follow the high command? Why defeat an enemy? Why be good even? Why not do whatever you want?"

Fred stared. "Look, religious or not, you have to admit the Germans and the Japanese need to be run out of town. It doesn't take a belief in God to come to that conclusion."

"But why? What good does it do?"

"Maybe because your God didn't do a good enough job of keeping the bad guys from killing innocent people. Maybe He needs a little help running them out of town, maybe even off this earth." Fred muttered a few more choice words. "Anyway, what are we gonna do with these green GIs, Captain? Where do you plan on taking them, since we still need to plot out the climbing routes?"

Nick folded the map. "They are going to work on the tower with the other officers. You and I are going on a scouting mission come morning. We can head out early tomorrow, scout the route, and lay in the pitons."

"You mean by ourselves? What about that mountain dame who wanted to help?"

Nick pondered that silently. He would dearly love a guide, and yes, he wouldn't mind if it were Lucy. She seemed so eager to lend a hand. He recalled her large eyes, dark brown and misty, her lips parted, her cheeks colored pink, looking as if she might guide him to the ends of the earth if he asked. Maybe it was just infatuation on her part, as Fred claimed. Right now he was only interested in what needed to be done. His duty, the duty of seeing these men trained for whatever mission the military sent them to complete. And if Lucy could help him accomplish this task, so be it.

He shook his head at Fred's inquiry, which bordered on teasing. "We have a map of the region. We know enough about climbing. We can figure out where to go, at least for now."

Fred chuckled. "I'm sure you would love an escort, but I guess we'll do what needs to be done."

Nick folded the map. "Lucy seems very intelligent and helpful, but that's it."

"You sure about that, sir? You two were getting along really well the other day."

"I was only feeding her interest in our operation. Nothing more. Remember, we need to keep the residents happy, to make friends when we can. We are invaders in their valley, so to speak. We need them on our side to be successful here. And as you well know, Lucy has a boyfriend who doesn't lack in his opinions." Nick began filling a green canvas backpack with some supplies. "So what do you say we head out early tomorrow morning and scout out the route?"

"I'm at your command," Fred acknowledged with a half-hearted salute.

Nick frowned. He hoped in the coming days Fred would show him the respect deserving of his rank now that the men had arrived. He hadn't minded the laxness in previous adventures together. They had been through quite a bit, from the time they both were caught on the mountain in a Colorado blizzard and survived in a snow cave. There Nick had thrown titles and rank to the wind. But this was different. The men would be watching their every move when it came to tackling the rocks, especially when it came to respecting the chain of command and following orders. Leadership and discipline were crucial to making all this work. That and plenty of prayer.

❧

Nick lay in his tent that night, listening to the raindrops splatter on the canvas like tiny feet. In one corner of the tent, the dampness had already begun to seep inside. Fred elected to stay in a separate tent rather than force Nick to share it with a lowly enlisted man, as he put it. Nick wanted to tell Fred to come join him but knew the separate quarters were in keeping with protocol now that the soldiers had arrived. Still, he missed the man's camaraderie and their conversations about their adventures in Colorado. Nick found himself alone in this massive tent with only his thoughts to keep him company as the rain fell harder.

He rolled over on the narrow cot, careful not to tumble to the ground below. He could think of more pleasant places to be, especially when stuck in a tent that did not keep the elements at bay. But he'd suffered through worse in his life. Like the snow shelter he once constructed to stay alive. Or the other tents he'd found himself in, perched on some rocky outcropping high in the Colorado Rockies, wondering if he might be found frozen to death come morning.

All were part of his survival skills and training that had eventually led him to the Mountain Training Group. He loved the adventure, but he wondered where it was taking him on this path of life and where he would end up. This could very well provide Nick his ticket to the front, from what he had been hearing. Rumors flew that the United States would soon become embroiled in the war in Europe. Already troops were beginning to amass in Britain once their training was completed. It would be a long and nasty conflict, driving a fierce enemy from lands it had conquered over the last few years. There was no time to think about life here. Like relationships. Marriage. Family. It seemed so out of reach, even if the conversations with Lucy and seeing a glimpse of her home life brought it to the forefront of his mind. The war did affect some of the people here but not nearly as much as those training for it. Lucy, her young man, and the other members of her family lived their lives apart from it all. Certainly the army's presence gave them a taste of reality. But Lucy didn't seem to mind having them here. In fact, she was quite willing to embrace it as part of life, and Nick with it.

The wind began to shake the tent. Raindrops flew and settled on him. He pulled the scratchy wool blanket over his head to protect himself from the dampness. If only he had the materials to construct a barracks. But that was impractical, given the short amount of time they had here. He wondered then what Donna would say about his rustic accommodations. He could picture her face wrinkling up, her nose in the air.

"This is perfectly awful, Nick!" she would say. "How can you sleep in some tent with the rain leaking in and everything? You'll catch your death of cold, maybe even come down with pneumonia or something."

And then he imagined Lucy's reaction.

"Here, Captain Landers. This is just what you need." She

would then produce a large umbrella to situate over his head.

Nick laughed in spite of his circumstances. *Yes, that's exactly what she would do.* And the next day she would trudge alongside him, through the muck and the mire created by the rains, then across the swollen river to the rocks that she loved. Maybe he should seek out her help. So it wasn't very becoming for her to tag along with two rough men. But acting as their guide, it wouldn't be so unseemly. She knew the Seneca Rocks area. He could learn a great deal and make the time here easier.

The rain finally began to let up, but Nick still felt damp. The situation was not pleasant, but his thoughts were. Thoughts of Lucy warmed him more than anything he could think of at that moment.

The next morning, bright sunshine greeted Nick as he emerged from the tent, tired from the lack of sleep and a night of contemplation. Fred met up with him, toting his backpack, ready for the scouting expedition to the rocks.

"All they have is baby food around here this morning," Fred grumbled, referring to the cereal issued for the breakfast. "What I wouldn't give for a plate of ham and eggs. Bet the families around here know how to put on a good meal. How about that mountain dame's family? Maybe we can head over there, plead starvation, and ask them to give us some good food? I mean, she likes you and all."

Nick said nothing as he adjusted the belt around his waist that contained the equipment for the day's expedition. He slipped a pair of binoculars over his head.

"You gonna eat anything, Captain? Can I get you some of that great food?"

"I'm not hungry," Nick said. "Just tired. The tent leaked last night."

Fred hooted. "You should have stayed in that warm building in Elkins with all the other COs, Captain. You'd be living it up just fine."

"Then I wouldn't be available to accomplish our mission here. Let's get going."

Fred shrugged and accompanied him. A mist hung over the open fields beyond the encampment. Sunshine made the droplets of rain glisten like jewels on the grass. The scents of the land came out in full force after the rains. Everything was fresh and new. If Nick must suffer through a drenching night in a soggy tent to witness the wonder of a new day, he didn't mind the storm in the least.

"Land ho!" Fred suddenly called out.

Nick readied his binoculars. "What? Did you find something already?"

"At ten o'clock, Captain. See for yourself."

Nick looked through the binoculars. First he saw woods, the grassy fields, and then a few cows. Working among the cows, he saw two figures in overalls. "What about it?"

"Looks like mountain people to me. Maybe even that dame you like so much. And it looks like she's ready to lead you into the wild blue yonder after all."

Nick handed the binoculars to Fred. "Take a look for yourself, Sergeant. Looks to me like two young fellows doing their morning chores." He began to walk swiftly across the field, refusing to glance back at the cattle or the people hard at work, hoping he would appear invisible. Right now he had a job to do. "Let's keep going. Hopefully, they won't see us."

"Mister! Hey, mister!" a young voice shouted from across the field.

Fred eyed Nick. A smile crept across his face. "So much for

slipping past unnoticed, Captain."

Two young boys ran swiftly toward them, their eyes wide. "Are you the men who are gonna climb the rocks?" one asked breathlessly.

"In a few days. Right now we're just doing some scouting and topography work."

The boy scrunched up his face. "What's that mean?"

"We're finding out the lay of the land, elevation changes, things like that." Nick withdrew his map and compass. "These tools help us figure out where to go. Then we hope to find a good climbing route up the rocks."

"Wow. Hey, we know about the rocks 'cause we live here. I'm Carl Bland. This here's my younger brother, Tim."

Nick straightened in interest. "You wouldn't happen to be Lucy's brothers?"

"Sure are! Hey, are you the soldier she's taken a shine to?"

Fred chuckled, even as Nick felt his throat constrict and his face heat up. "I'm not sure what you mean by that. Your sister just stopped by the camp as a friendly gesture. There don't seem to be that many friendly faces around here."

"Lucy's real friendly. You don't have to worry about that. So are you heading to the rocks up there?"

"Yep, got some routes we need to plan out. We'll be taking the men climbing very soon."

"Wish I could do that," Carl said wistfully. "You think you could teach me how to rock climb sometime?"

Nick smiled. "Wish we could, young fellow, but as it is we have our hands full with these enlisted men, many of whom are not happy about climbing. I think it will take us time to get them acquainted to it all. The techniques, the equipment. . ."

The boys began peppering them with questions about the

equipment needed to scale the rocks. Nick shook his head, explaining that they needed to get going, but maybe sometime they would like to come and watch one of the exercises.

The boys' faces brightened at this suggestion. "Sure thing!" they both said at once. "That would be great."

When the two boys had scampered off, Fred laughed long and loud, as if he had just witnessed a great comedy act. "It seems to me, my dear captain, that you are linked to this Bland family in more ways than one. There's just no escaping them, is there?"

Nick wanted to contradict Fred but could not. In fact, he couldn't help silently agreeing.

five

Lucy wiped the sweat from her face, which had already begun accumulating from the warm summer day. Momma had given her instructions to do the gardening that Lucy had allowed to slip these past few days. Not that she wanted to admit her preoccupation, but ever since the soldiers had arrived in the valley, her thoughts turned to them night and day. When she arrived home from the personal tour Nick had given her of the camp, Momma immediately confronted her, especially at seeing the rip in the knee of her overalls.

"What are you doing, Lucy? First you get your overalls wet, and now they're ripped."

Lucy looked at the tear in dismay, realizing she must have done it on that corncrib or beehive or whatever the contraption was that Nick showed her. If he had let her, she would have proven herself on the thing, showing him there was more to her name than Bland, that she could do whatever he asked of her and more. Perhaps she could still convince Nick to allow her to help them navigate the rocks, if he would just forget the notion that having her along was unseemly. She was up to the challenge. Maybe if she convinced him of her outdoor skill, he would think her worthy enough to pursue. Maybe he would suggest an outing to the picture show or the soda fountain in Petersburg.

Lucy stuttered as she tried to explain to her mother how she had ripped her overalls unknowingly. Lucy then fetched the sewing box and immediately set about mending the tear. "I think I'd rather wear dresses from now on," she informed Momma. "Overalls are getting too hot with summer here."

"You *are* going to wear overalls when you do the gardening, aren't you? I need the last of the broccoli picked today and the tomatoes hoed. The weeds are already crowding them in."

Lucy sighed in exasperation. At times she wished she had her own home to look after. She was twenty, after all. Plenty old enough to be married and caring for a place. Staying here with two rambunctious brothers underfoot and being under the watchful eyes of her parents was getting to be too much. When would they allow her to venture out on her own, to make something of her life? She'd once asked Daddy if he would teach her how to drive, hoping it would give her some freedom. He thought up some excuse, even suggesting that Allen could teach her one day, maybe after they had tied the knot.

Lucy cut off a large broccoli head and placed it in the basket. She shivered at the thought. Marrying Allen was the farthest thing from her mind. She hoped that somehow his business at Elkins would keep him beyond the week he had said he would be gone. *What a thought, Lucy,* she chastised herself. *Allen has been a good friend.* A good friend, yes, but never a man like Nick. Dear Nick, broad-shouldered and handsome, standing there in his gray T-shirt. She sighed. *A picture-perfect man with whom to spend a lifetime.*

"Lu, hey, Lu!" a voice cried out.

Lucy twisted around to see Carl running up with Tim following close behind. "You know you're never supposed to call me Lu!" she shouted back, picking up the basket of broccoli heads to take back to the house.

"Ha! Then I won't tell you who we saw today in the pasture."

She hesitated. "Who?"

Carl gave her a sheepish grin. "Wouldn't you like to know? What will you give me if I tell you?"

"How about I tell Daddy what you're up to and let him tan your britches?"

"You don't scare me, old Lu-Lu. If you knew who it was we talked to, you'd be hightailing it over there faster than any jackrabbit. Wouldn't she, Tim?" He poked his younger brother.

"What, you mean that soldier she likes?"

Carl pushed him. "You weren't supposed to blab! It was our secret."

Lucy nearly dropped the basket. "You mean you saw Nick? I mean, Captain Landers?"

"I don't know his name. There were two of them. They were gonna go scout out the rocks."

"What did he look like, Tim?" She coddled her youngest brother. "C'mon. Buy you a grape soda at the store if you tell me."

"Don't say a thing," Carl warned.

"He wasn't anyone special," Tim said. "Just some soldier. But he asked if we were your brothers. And he talked about you visiting the camp. When did you go, anyway? And how come you didn't take me? I'd love to see everything, like the guns and trucks and stuff."

Lucy never answered his question. Instead she raced back to the house, forgetting everything, even the basket of broccoli and the faint voice of Tim asking when she was going to buy him that bottle of grape soda. *This might be my only chance to see Nick while he is scouting the rocks. I know he doesn't want me there, but if I go, he'll have no choice but to let me come along. Then I'll get to spend more time with him.* She struggled out of the overalls and blouse, rushing into the bathroom to wash up. Her face was marred by dirt. Dark circles surrounded her eyes from her sleepless night of reminiscing about the encounter at the camp. Every waking moment seemed to be filled with visions of Nick Landers. Why, she didn't know. This might give her the opportunity to find out. She had to know if God was drawing them together or if she truly was lost in a maze of wild emotion.

Lucy threw open the doors to the wardrobe and settled on a navy print dress. No overalls for this venture. She must look nice if she had any hope of grabbing his attention. She fingered the material for a moment before slipping it over her head. She and Momma had sewn the dress for church wear. She loved the way the skirt flared and the belt accentuated her slim waist. She hoped Nick would love it, too.

Lucy picked up her purse, ready to head down the stairs, when she suddenly stopped. *What am I doing? Those men are heading for the rocks. How can I climb a hillside wearing a dress?* She sighed in exasperation and returned to her room. Reluctantly she put her blouse back on, then the overalls, even though they were covered in dirt from her work in the garden and had a mended knee. This is how she would appear to Nick—Lucy Bland, in her customary overalls, her hair tied up in two ponytails, but with a heart willing to do anything for him. She hoped he would look beyond her appearance to what lay inside.

At the last moment she sighted the blueberry muffins she had made for breakfast. One by one she put them in a basket when Carl and Tim rushed into the kitchen.

"Hey, I'm hungry," Tim shouted.

"Don't take them all, Lu!" Carl protested. "Give me some."

"Here, you can each have one. I'm taking them over to the soldiers. I'm sure they have a hankering for some fresh baked goods. Army food must be nasty."

"You just want that Nick person to turn sweet on you," Carl said, spitting out muffin crumbs as he spoke.

"And you just want to make a nuisance out of yourself."

"At least we told you about him," Carl reminded her. "Or rather Tim spilled the beans about it."

"Yeah, and you still have to buy me a grape soda, Lu," Tim added, his mouth full of muffin.

"You keep calling me Lu and you won't get anything." She covered the basket with a hand towel. "Don't tell Momma where I've gone." She knew that wouldn't happen, but she still hoped to avoid more confrontations, especially where her mother was concerned.

On her way down the road, she waved to a passerby riding a bicycle. Above her, Seneca Rocks reigned supreme with the gray and black stone against the backdrop of a sapphire sky. She envisioned herself and Nick perched near those rocks, singing a hymn to God and enjoying each other's company. "Rock of Ages" would seem appropriate.

Lucy paused. She hadn't even considered whether Nick was a Christian. Momma talked a great deal about finding a husband who trusted in their Lord and Savior. She had no idea if Nick felt the same way. If he didn't, what would she do?

I'll just have to convince him, that's all. Invite him to church. Have the pastor speak to him. Pray like crazy. She grew nervous just thinking about it. How sad it would be if she found out he wasn't a Christian and all this had been in vain. The feelings she had. The sleepless nights. The blueberry muffins that Momma was sure to wonder about when she found them missing, knowing that sugar was a prized commodity. *He must be a Christian,* she reasoned. *He is a nice and courteous man, after all.* Lucy knew quite well that being nice didn't make one a Christian, not by any means. As the pastor often said, "No one does good, not one. All our works are but filthy rags, lest you've put your faith in the Lord Jesus." Yet there were things about Nick that led her to believe he might be. *Oh, Lord, I pray Nick has put his faith in Jesus. Lord, please show me his true heart.*

Lucy looked up at the rocks, wondering where the men might have gone. She sighed, hoping her brothers hadn't made up some wild tale about meeting the men. She wouldn't put it past them to do such a thing, especially the way Carl had been teasing her these last few days. Lucy searched for a place to ford the North Fork River, choosing the same rocky area where she had taken a spill before meeting Nick. Using a large stick, Lucy maneuvered her way across the slippery rocks, some teetering beneath her feet. She murmured a quick prayer for safety and, in particular, the safety of the muffins she was sure would win Nick's heart. Once across, she ventured up the foot trail she and Allen had used many times to access the viewpoint just below the summit of Seneca Rocks. There she caught sight of two military men about halfway up the hillside, surveying the terrain.

Suddenly they wheeled about. To her astonishment, one drew a pistol and aimed it in her direction. "Who goes there? Identify yourself!"

Lucy froze for an instant. She dropped her stick and scampered back down the trail, too scared to even think.

"Put that away!" a voice shouted. She then heard, "Wait a minute!" echo down to her, accompanied by the sound of footsteps.

Her limbs shook. Perspiration dripped down her face. Dizzy and weak from fright, she felt she might faint. *Don't look back! Oh, God, please help me! Please don't let him shoot me.*

"Lucy? Lucy, please wait!"

She heard her name and stopped. The voice belonged to Nick. His face was etched with concern. "I'm sorry about that. Fred overreacted. Guess he's getting ready to meet the Germans or something."

"Like there are enemies around here, Captain L–Landers," she sputtered, trying to catch her breath. "How can you scare a person like that?"

"I didn't even know Fred had his pistol on him. Please, it's all right."

She plopped down on a rock by the edge of the river, breathing rapidly. "I've never had a gun pointed at me," she murmured, wiping a stray tear from her face. "Daddy would go hunting, but that was just to get a critter or two. I'm not used to all this, you men in your uniforms, pointing guns, making wooden towers. It's like what Allen said. We've been invaded."

"I'm sorry, Lucy," he said again. A second pair of footsteps approached—Nick's friend Fred, whom Lucy was beginning to dislike more and more.

"You scared her to death," Nick told him.

"Well, she sure didn't do anything to announce herself, Captain. Sorry about that."

Fred had tucked the pistol back into its holster, but Lucy couldn't keep her eyes off it, wondering if he really would have used it on her.

"I didn't know I had to announce myself in my own home-town and in my own country," she told the man flatly. "After all, you're the ones who are trespassing here with your trucks and your tents everywhere. Now you're pointing guns at civilians."

"Well, if you had just—"

"Sergeant Watkins, do you mind?" Nick interrupted. "We left our topography materials up there on the ridge. Go ahead and finish plotting the trail on the map, and I'll catch up with you."

Fred stared at Nick, then Lucy. He gave a stiff salute, wheeled on one foot, and marched back up the hill. Lucy dried one last tear as Nick slid onto a rock beside her.

"I'm sorry again for what happened, Lucy. I hope you'll forgive us."

His close proximity and gentle words imparted comfort. *Nick, I would forgive everything, especially if you put your huge arms around me.* She cast the thought aside and surveyed the river flowing gently by on its way to a much larger river. Actually, she was glad his friend had pointed the pistol. She soaked in Nick's concern for her like parched ground absorbing the gentle rain. How nice it was to have someone so apologetic and caring sitting close beside her. If only she knew what else made up the man who called himself Nick Landers. What were his hopes and dreams? His plans? He had an aura of ruggedness about him, as if the mountains and he were one. He was bold and adventuresome. He scaled great heights. He camped out in blizzards. But what were his thoughts on life? And love? And did he trust in the Lord of heaven and earth?

"You look like you're deep in thought," he observed. "I'm not sure what else I can say to calm your worry. Unfortunately, you will probably see more things around here that might alarm you. We are instructed to take the utmost care among the civilians. We will only do what is necessary but with your safety in mind. I know the display you saw doesn't give you much confidence, but I hope my apology helps in some way."

"It helps a little, thanks." She opened the basket to show him the blueberry muffins. "I thought army food might be getting to you right about now, so I brought these."

"Why, thank you!" he said with enthusiasm, helping himself. "This is terrific."

"So you really like to rock climb?" she suddenly asked, picking up a rock and tossing it into the river.

"I love it. I've scaled plenty of rocks, some a lot more challenging than these here. I just have to convince the new GIs that they can do it, too."

"Where else have you climbed?"

"The Rocky Mountains. That's where I'm from. Colorado to be exact."

"I've never been anywhere except here. I've studied other parts of the country, in school. Someday I would like to see the ocean and many other places. But I don't know if I will ever leave here."

"Why not? You have to leave sometime. There's so much to see. God made a great place when He made the United States. Maybe you'll even get to Colorado someday."

Lucy inhaled a swift breath, glancing at him out of the corner of her eye to see the sincerity in his face. He had mentioned God. Not that this was a sign of his Christianity, but at least he didn't shun the name of God. He spoke it quite naturally, in fact. *Oh, Lord, can it be? Is he a Christian?* "I know I often think about how God made Seneca Rocks. The rocks here are different compared to other mountains. They look more like scales on a lizard."

Nick chuckled. He glanced over his shoulder, toward the rocks high on the hillside behind them. "It is amazing. I think of the Rocky Mountains, too; a whole line of them with ridges one after the other in a rippling effect. On the summits it can snow year-round."

"You talked about staying in some kind of snow shelter. I can't even imagine it, though I know some Eskimos way up north live in igloos. Imagine, homes built out of big blocks of ice. Did you ever want to live like that?"

Nick laughed. "No. A snow shelter for one night is enough for me. As it is, I do miss a good, sturdy shelter. My tent leaked during the storm last night—made me wish for a solid roof over my head."

Lucy shook her head. "That's awful. Once our roof leaked, and Daddy was up there at once, fixing it. Thankfully only the rug got wet. I can't imagine sleeping in a damp bed. Were you cold?"

"No, fortunately it's summer. I wouldn't have wanted it to be leaking during freezing weather, though."

Lucy fell silent, thinking of Nick shivering in some cold, leaky tent. "Wish I'd known—I would've brought you an umbrella," she remarked.

His sudden laugher made her jerk around in a start. "Now that is very funny, Lucy. I have to admit, while I was lying there, I thought about that very thing. What's the one thing Lucy Bland might have brought me in a storm like this? A good old umbrella to hide under."

Lucy stared in amazement and awe. Nick had been thinking about her in his time of trial, with the rain beating above his head and leaking over his bed? This was more than she could have hoped or dreamed. *Oh, God, I'm in heaven. Just to know that Nick thought of me coming to his aid.* And here she thought she'd made a feeble impression on him that day in the camp. More of a nuisance than anything. He must have seen something redeeming in her, worthy enough to think of her in the darkest night as if she were a lamp set high on a hill.

Nick looked sheepishly toward the river. He sat there in quiet contemplation while the river rushed by. "Ever go fishing?" he finally asked.

"Sometimes. We get trout mostly. Sometimes bass."

Again they sat in silence until a holler came from the hillside. "Sounds like my sergeant found something good," he said, slowly standing to his feet.

"I could take you up to the viewpoint near the top of the rocks," she offered once more. "You can see the whole valley from there. I know the way."

"How about you point me in the right direction?"

"Okay. Follow the trail you've been on. You'll come to a fork. Take the right trail. It starts getting kind of steep just before it comes out on the rocks."

"So the trail only goes to the top of the rocks?"

"Well, not all the way to the top. The rocks are too narrow at the top for that. But it does end at a pretty viewpoint. You can see everything."

"I was also hoping for a trail that went to the base where the rocks begin. The sergeant and I were going to check out climbing routes up the rock faces. The pitches I talked about on our tour, remember, where you need ropes to climb?"

"You'll have to go downriver for that, beyond where the cattle are grazing. Another trail goes to just below the rocks. I haven't been there in a long time, though. I always go to the viewpoint."

"Thanks, Lucy. Without you, this whole day might have been wasted. Though I'm sure the view from up top is great, we do need to check out the other trail." He stretched his arms over his head. "I'd better go find my sergeant." She watched Nick ascend the trail effortlessly, calling for his companion. He was tall and strong, like a great tree gripping the hillside, unmoved by the wind and rain. She thought of leaving them to their venture and returning home but instead waited for them to come down. Even if he didn't want her guiding them to the rocks, she could still show him the cut-off trail. Maybe one day all this would point the way for his heart.

When the men came stumbling back down the trail, Fred complained of twisting his ankle on the steep terrain. "If this is any idea of what we have to face, Captain, I'm not sure anyone is going to be able to do it."

"Of course you will," Lucy said, standing to her feet. "If I can do it, anybody can."

Fred glanced over at her, his face flushed. "Didn't realize you were standing there, missy. I thought you'd gone back to your horses and cattle."

"I thought maybe I could at least show you where the trail is, Captain Landers. If that's all right."

Nick nodded. "That's a good idea since Sergeant Watkins here probably couldn't make it if we had to traipse around looking for it."

"Old Sergeant Fred is just fine and dandy, Captain sir, even if my ankle is a little sore. I can do whatever you need." He shook his leg and began to cross the river, followed by Lucy and Nick.

Lucy felt Nick close behind her, like a strong shield ready to protect her from harm. How she wished he would suggest a date somewhere—to the theater or even a walk in the cool of the evening. Instead, he waited on her as she led the way downriver. "I haven't been there much," she said. "Maybe once or twice." She paused, pointing to a trail opposite the river. "There it is. Sorry you have to cross back over the river again. And there aren't many stepping-stones, so it will be deeper here."

"We should have stayed on the opposite side of the bank and bushwhacked to the trail," Fred grumbled. He plodded headlong back into the river. Water nearly came up to his knees. "Always wanted to see if my boots could float. Guess they'll get a good test."

"Thanks for your help, Lucy," Nick offered with a smile.

Lucy sucked in her breath at the sweet way he said her name. Gently, with tenderness. Without even thinking she blurted out, "Do you ever get time off, Captain Landers? Like in the evenings? I mean, I'm sure Momma would be happy to have you over for dinner sometime. Daddy would like to hear any news you have about the war."

He hesitated, then shook his head. "With the recruits here, I'd better stick close to camp until everything is set with them. But thanks for the invitation."

Lucy dug her hands into the pockets of her overalls, hoping to conceal her disappointment. "Oh, sure, I understand." She gave a lopsided smile as he began his trek across the river in pursuit of his friend. *Lucy, why couldn't you be more patient?* she lamented silently. *Now he thinks you're some brazen woman.* All the encouraging thoughts she'd had about their encounter quickly faded. She tried not to let the tears surface as she turned away, refusing to look back at the men. *God, maybe we are too different and this is just a silly dream of mine. But, oh, I do like him. Only You can make my dream come true, if I'm patient enough to let You do the work. Dear Lord, help me wait on Your timing.*

six

Patience was a virtue, or so she had been taught. Patience when life threw curve balls and she was trying to catch them. Patience with Nick Landers. Ever since meeting him, Lucy felt like she was chasing curve balls. While she believed Nick did have an interest in her, at the same time he held himself back, as if unwilling to move forward. Maybe he already had a girl back in Colorado. Or he wondered about Allen. Or because he knew he would only be here a few weeks and pursuing a relationship was not something he had the time or the will to do. If only she could read his thoughts and determine where his true feelings lie. After all, she had been in his thoughts that rainy night. She perceived a sincere look in his eye and heard the gentleness in his voice. She cupped her cheek with her hand. Maybe all this was some dream without any basis in reality. But to her, Nick Landers couldn't be more genuine, even if she still knew very little about him. If only she could discover more.

Lucy contemplated seeking him out again, but Momma had given her a list of unending chores to complete. More weeding in the garden. Mending the boys' socks. Going over to the store for some staples. She left that errand for last. Any day now Allen would be returning from his errand in Elkins. She hardly knew what she'd say if she saw him, even though she had agreed to meet with him when he returned. What if he sensed something was going on in her heart—that she had grown interested in another man? How would he react to such news?

Lucy didn't want to think about it as she unwound more thread to fix a hole in Tim's sock. Thankfully, Momma had gotten the boys out of her hair, charging them with the duty of cleaning out the barn. At times she thought she could hear them arguing. No doubt Carl was upset that Tim wasn't pulling his weight, as often happened when they worked together.

"You seem quiet today," Momma observed.

Lucy looked up. She hadn't even heard her mother come in, so soft were her footsteps. Either that or Lucy was completely preoccupied. No doubt the latter. "Oh, just thinking."

"I heard Tim and Carl talking about some soldier, the one who came here a few days ago, looking for a guide. They said you've been sneaking out to see him?"

Lucy put down the mending. *I'm gonna get them for that,* she thought, pressing her lips tightly together. "Momma, all I've been doing is making sure they know their way around here. That's why they came to the house the other day. They had no idea how to get to the base of the rocks, so I just showed them the trail."

"Hmm. That's not what Carl says, but he's also known to make up some interesting stories."

"Yes, he does." She returned to the mending, hoping her mother wouldn't notice her heated face.

"I do wish, though, that you had let Daddy know about them wanting to find the trails. I don't like the idea of you keeping company with men like that."

"They're just soldiers, Momma."

"Yes, but they are men, too. Far away from home and maybe

even looking for trouble. I've already heard about one soldier in Elkins and how he was going after a farmer's gal. I won't even say what happened. But you are not to go to the soldier camp alone anymore. It's too dangerous."

Lucy sighed. "Momma, it's all right."

"Yes, it will be all right if you stay here and don't go traipsing off by yourself, at least not until Allen returns and can escort you. By the way, isn't he supposed to be coming back soon? The week is nearly up."

"Something like that," she answered carelessly, tugging at the thread with the needle. Her mother stared at her thoughtfully before moving off into the kitchen. Lucy sighed and stood to her feet, throwing the socks into the mending basket. At least she could deal with one matter right now— her unruly brothers and their big mouths, which had nearly landed her in the middle of another firestorm.

Lucy heard the rise of young voices debating about the work inside the barn when she entered. In the darkness she nearly tripped over a pitchfork and rake. "What are you doing leaving these tools in the middle of the floor?" she shouted at them. "I could have hurt myself."

"Help me move this, Tim," Carl was saying, handling a wooden barrel.

Lucy came instead and helped Carl move it to the opposite side of the barn. "Now, would you like to tell me what you said to Momma about the soldiers?"

"Not a thing," he told her with a sly smile on his face.

"You know that isn't true, Carl Matthew. You've been blabbing to everyone about my business. And quite frankly, I'm getting tired of it."

"I just want to know when you plan on telling Allen that

you've got another boyfriend."

Lucy ground her teeth. "I do not have another boyfriend. I was only helping guide the men to the rocks—if it's any of your business."

"I could have done that myself," Carl retorted. "I know those rocks real well. I've even done some climbing myself. I could tell them everything they need to know."

"You have never climbed them."

"Have so. Not with equipment and stuff, but I've gone up them. I know a lot more than you know. I don't know why you'd want to help them except to take peeks at the captain there."

"You're impossible! I'm warning you right now not to be telling Momma or anyone else my business. Or I'll tell Daddy what I saw in your room the other day."

Carl stood with his arms crossed. "What? You didn't see nothing. You're making it up."

"You know very well. A cigarette." Lucy turned on her heel, preparing to head out into the yard when she heard Carl call for her.

"Don't you dare say anything about that," he hissed. "I wasn't gonna smoke it. I—I'm keeping it for a friend."

"Sure you are." She held out her hand. "I think we have an agreement, don't we?"

Carl stared at her hand as if it were on fire before reluctantly shaking it.

"And you'd better get rid of that cigarette, too. All it does is make your breath bad and make you sick. It isn't glamorous at all, even if a lot of people do it nowadays."

Lucy whirled and returned to the house. At least she could claim a small victory, but to what end, she remained uncertain.

She knew things were happening between her and Nick, and one day soon she would have to reconcile those feelings. For now she continued to dream about the future. *Captain and Mrs. Nicholas Landers. Mrs. Lucy Landers.* She paused. *Lucy Landers!* She shuddered. *Oh, no. Two Ls.* She giggled. It didn't matter. She would be proud to carry that name as his wife. If only she could convince Nick, or more importantly, if God could change his heart toward her. There must be something there, after all. Nick had thought of her during that long, dreary night in his tent. If that wasn't the beginning of love, what was? Since the moment he'd revealed that fact, Lucy had clung to his words, even when doubt began to creep in and she felt a million miles from him—though the camp was only a mile or two down the road. She would recall how he thought of her in his most depressing hour. The thought sustained her more than anything else.

But with Momma knowing of her trips and the boys sticking their noses into her business, she would have to be more careful. Maybe she could volunteer to take in the cattle on the pasture adjoining the camp. Or feign a need to go to Petersburg that would take her right by the camp on the main road. Or what about writing Nick a letter? Carl and Tim would never know about it. Nor would Momma. There must be errand boys running from the store or other places to keep the camp well stocked with supplies. She could write the letter and have someone deliver it. Or try sending it through the regular mail. *Oh, why didn't I think of this sooner?*

Lucy immediately went to her room to locate paper and a pencil. She hadn't written much since her school days, but this day, armed and ready, the words just flowed out of her very being.

My dearest Nick,

Oh, how I love to write those words because you are dear—dear to me, that is. I know you don't know much about me, but I feel like I have known you forever. And I do want us to be together. Whatever it takes, I want to become your wife. I would make you a wonderful home and be there for you always. No matter where we are or what happens, I am here for you and you alone.

Lucy paused to reread it. This type of letter would never do, at least in the stage they were in. She could just picture his reaction—his dark eyes widening, his cheeks turning ruddy as his sergeant friend teased him about some enraptured young woman of the hills with her claws in him. Lucy placed the letter in the drawer of her desk and took out another sheet of paper.

Dear Captain Landers,

I'm not sure when I will see you again, but I wanted to thank you for all you're doing for our country. It makes me proud when I see men like you here to protect us. I know the training on Seneca Rocks will go very well, because I'm sure you're very good at what you do. The men are blessed to have you. If you need anything, I know our family would be happy to help. Thank you also for the tour of the camp. Maybe we will be able to talk again before you leave.

Sincerely,
Lucy Bland

She read it over and sighed. Cordial and considerate if not bland-sounding, like her name. In no way did it reveal her true feelings, but at least nothing in it should cause him to turn away. Maybe it would be enough to draw a bit of interest, to let him know that she wasn't some lovesick girl waiting for him to sweep her into his arms and give her a kiss. Even if she did feel that way.

Lucy slid the letter into an envelope and addressed it with the words *Captain Nicholas Landers, Seneca Rocks Camp.* "Now to find someone at the Hoppers' store who can deliver this."

Lucy changed out of her overalls and into a dress. She didn't want to go to the store to deliver an important note looking like a ragamuffin. She checked her appearance. For all she knew, Nick might even come by the store and she could hand him the letter personally. Maybe he would suggest a picnic by the North Fork River as a thank-you. *My, how my imagination can run away with me.* For now, she would relish in whatever came of this letter, even if he were to simply smile or send his own note of thanks. Any sign of encouragement would be welcomed with open arms and an open heart.

Lucy quickly headed down the road toward the store. As usual, Seneca Rocks stood before her in all its beauty. She wondered if Nick was yet climbing the rocky pinnacles. Maybe even now he was looking down at her from some lofty perch, staring through his binoculars. Maybe he saw her in the navy print dress and thought to himself, *Now there's a sweet dish I'd like to take somewhere—maybe to the movie house in Petersburg.* Lucy sighed. *If only.*

She mounted the steps to the general store, nodding at several neighbors who bid her a good afternoon. Ed Hopper gave her a huge smile when he saw her. "You're in luck, Lucy."

Is Nick in here buying something? She nearly popped the question before stopping herself. How could she even think of asking Allen's father such a thing when he knew nothing of the man? "Why is that, Mr. Hopper?"

"Allen just got in this morning. In fact, I'll fetch him right now. He'll sure be glad to see you. It's been Lucy this, Lucy that."

Lucy stared, first at the open door where Mr. Hopper had exited, then at the letter still in her hand. She tucked the envelope hastily in the pocket of her dress, just before the door opened and Allen rushed in.

"Boy, how I missed you, Lucy!" he said, curling his arms around her. "And don't you look nice! Wow, what a greeting. Makes a fellar just want to come running home."

"Hi, Allen." She gave him a swift embrace before slowly stepping out of his arms. "So how was the trip to Elkins?"

"Boring, but don't tell Daddy I said that," he whispered. He took her hand, gently escorting her outside. "I just did the normal things. Checked out inventory for the store to see what's available and what isn't anymore with the war going on. But boy, Elkins is hopping."

"What do you mean?"

"Soldiers. I mean they are everywhere. It's like an invasion. In the stores. On the road. Asking directions. Some even had guns. I saw a few who claimed they belonged to that camp by Seneca Rocks." He looked beyond the parking lot of the store to the rocks. "I see they already have some kind of tent city set up down there."

Lucy tentatively touched the letter in her pocket. "Yes, they do."

"Have you been back there? What's going on?"

"Oh, nothing much. They plan on climbing the rocks. A couple of them came around asking if you wanted to help them find some climbing routes. In fact, they were the same two soldiers we met that day by the river."

Allen raised his eyebrow. "You mean the ones who drove that truck over my dad's land? I thought they would've hightailed it in the other direction after the meeting we had. Like I would show them where to climb. Ha!"

"Allen, they're only doing it to help our country. Nick says it's to train for the war in Europe. They are not here to cause harm but to help."

Allen stared at her quietly for moment or two. "Sounds to me like you've had more than just a little one- or two-word conversation with these GIs."

"Well, they came by the house, looking for a guide. What was I supposed to do, ignore them? I mean, they're fighting for our country. I think they deserve as much help and respect as we can give them."

"Well, I'm helping, too," Allen said defensively. "Trying to make sure you still have sugar and other supplies before they're all gone. And speaking of that, I got something for you while I was in Elkins."

Lucy prayed with all her might it wouldn't be what she feared. When he returned with a thin square package, she breathed a sigh of relief.

"I heard from some other shopkeepers that this kind of thing will soon be gone," Allen was saying as she opened the package to reveal a pair of nylons. "All the women like 'em and they are getting scarce. So I thought you'd want some. Got some for your mother, too, and mine."

"Thank you, Allen. That's real sweet of you." She gave him her best smile, all the while thinking what Nick would say if he saw her in a pretty dress complete with nylons and heels.

She pushed away such a thought as Allen continued to stare at her.

"You look like you're a million miles away. So, are you up for going to Petersburg? We still have to finish where we left off when I had to leave for Elkins."

Lucy swallowed hard. "Actually, Allen, I have some chores to finish up at home."

"I'm sure that can wait. Especially if your mother knows I just got home. If you want, I'll go and ask her if it's all right."

Lucy bit her lip, imagining her brothers coming out of the barn to greet Allen and then spouting off to him what had happened this past week. She could see his ears turning red and a slow rage building inside him. Even if she did make an agreement with Carl not to say anything, Tim was known to speak up at the least provocation. He would tell Allen how she had sneaked out to the camp a couple of times to visit the soldiers. And she knew Allen would be upset if he found out. He wouldn't understand one bit. Oh, how she wanted to break down and tell him the truth—that she had fallen in love with Nick Landers, a man with hopes and dreams, a dazzling smile, and laughter that warmed her heart. But compared to Allen, she still knew so little about Nick. And she didn't know where Nick's heart stood, either. For now, any confession must wait.

"Really, I do need to finish the list Momma gave me to do," she said instead. "Maybe we can go another day. After all, you just got back from one trip. I don't think you'd want to leave on another."

"Believe me, this is a trip I've wanted to take for a very long time." He picked up her hand. "Maybe I should just come right out and say it now rather than later."

"Here?" She looked about nervously as customers drove up,

exchanging friendly chatter with each other or heading into the store to make their purchases.

"You're right, this isn't a good place," he agreed. "Okay, we'll settle on a place and then I'll have your attention at last. What day?"

"What day?" Lucy repeated. Suddenly she caught sight of the mailman coming to pick up the daily mail. Again her hand tentatively touched the letter. "Excuse me just a minute, Allen." She rushed over to deposit the letter in the man's pouch. "I don't really have an address for this person," she told the man, "but he's at the army camp by Seneca Rocks."

"Just so long as his name's on it and he's at that camp, it will get to him."

Lucy nodded. When she returned, Allen was pacing with his hands stuffed inside the pockets of his trousers, looking at her curiously.

"That's one errand done," she said nonchalantly. "I almost forgot to mail the letter."

"Anyway, what day should we get together for our outing, Lucy? How about Friday?"

Lucy thought hard and fast. She could agree to a date and then have something come up. At least it would give her some time to think up a good excuse, if not the truth. Besides, if she didn't agree on a day, Allen would only grow suspicious that something had happened during his absence. She sighed. If only she were more confident about her chances with Nick, that he liked her as much as she liked him. But without that confidence, she had nothing to hold on to and everything to lose. And she didn't want to lose it all. "I think Friday will be good, but I'll have to let you know if something suddenly comes up."

"That's an interesting answer, but I guess I'll take it for what it's worth." He again took her hand. His thumb stroked her skin. "I really did miss you, Lucy. At least I won't have to go away now for a long time."

Lucy glanced back toward Seneca Rocks, hoping he wouldn't try to kiss her like that day on the porch. There was no doubt Allen was a sweet guy. She cherished their friendship, their rambles, and the times they played in the river or took walks up to the rocks. But she could not let go of the fact that he was just a friend to her. And in his absence she had met an honest-to-goodness man of flesh and bone with a kind spirit she loved. "You really are a million miles away," he said again. "Well, I need to go talk to Dad about the trip. I'll stop by and see you when I can. Hopefully next time we'll be able to talk more."

Lucy watched him meander back to the store, his head low, his feet scuffing up the dirt, clearly vexed by their meeting. She did feel bad misleading him like this. If only she could be sure about everything, that God would clear these muddy rivers, that she would know which direction to turn. *Oh, God, I need to know somehow.* She took to her feet then, slowly continuing her walk down the road, gazing transfixed at the rocks before her and then the tiny green army tents in the distance. No doubt Nick had his hands full with all the new soldiers. She wondered if he had managed to find the routes he needed up to the rocks. She wondered, too, if he'd had time to think about her in the midst of his duty.

Just then she heard a whistle of appreciation. A truckload of soldiers came rattling down the road, some of them waving and calling out. Lucy looked away shyly. All this attention was new to her. Nick would never do anything so unseemly, but if he did whistle, it would be fine with her. It would give her something else to hold on to. *At least you will read the letter,* she thought, stooping to pluck a daisy by the side of the road. She twirled the flower in her fingers. *I would love to have sent you the first version, but maybe appreciation and encouragement will be enough to make something happen and soon. . .before Friday comes.*

seven

Nick glanced down at his dinner that night at the mess tent. He refused to say what others called the monstrosity served up on the aluminum plates—the slivers of dried beef in some sauce that tasted like wallpaper paste, all thrown over dry bread. Fred was quick to make the first comment about the unmentionable stuff served "on a shingle," and in front of the men, much to Nick's disgust. For himself, Nick stole away with the plate in hand, eating only a few bites before dumping the rest on the ground for the critters to consume. In no time a stray dog came wandering about the camp and ate Nick's meal in two huge gulps. Nick laughed, watching the hound lick his lips and wag his tail in the hope of a second helping.

"Believe me, you don't want to eat any more of that stuff," he told the dog. He missed the meals he'd enjoyed back at Camp Hale in Colorado. Sometimes it would be hearty beef steaks right off the Colorado range. Or chicken. Real beef stew. Chili. The cooks here were still trying to get adequate supplies lined up from the local farms. He had seen a few trucks come by with fresh produce. Maybe things would turn around and good meals would soon be forthcoming.

Right now Nick's stomach rumbled at the thought of Lucy's blueberry muffins. He missed them now more than ever. If only she would come by with a new batch, hot out of the oven, accompanied by her shy smile and dressed in her overalls as if ready for a ramble. Sometimes he would go out to the sentry post, salute the guards on duty, and casually search the neighboring fields with his binoculars for any sign of her. Much to his dismay, he always came up empty. He decided he had put her off that day by the river. She had been nice enough to invite him to a meal at her folks' place. Now he regretted not jumping up and agreeing to a wonderful home-cooked meal and with a real family to boot. What was he thinking? Even if she might have some kind of infatuation for him, what did it matter? Instead he had to contend with lousy camp food, Fred's obnoxious ways, and the green GIs commenting on the wooden tower they had to climb and wondering why they were forced to do things beyond their capability.

Nick came to his feet and again headed toward the sentry post. They would wonder what he was up to, most likely. He assured them, as he did most evenings, that nothing was amiss, and then he ventured beyond the camp perimeter to the fencing that separated the camp from the pasture. This night the fields were empty. The Bland boys must have finished their chores early. He wondered what their mother gave them to eat for dinner tonight. Maybe slices of smoked ham and heaps of mashed sweet potatoes that they washed down with cups of fresh milk.

Get a hold of yourself, Nick. Bad food is part of army life. But he couldn't get used to it, not after Lucy had begun spoiling him. And how did he return her favor? A slap on her wrist by some dissuading comment. Maybe he had offered a smile or two, but little else to show her how much her kind ways had affected him. Especially now when he had nothing.

"There you are!" a voice startled him. He turned to see Fred, still holding a plate of the evening fare, gobbling it down as if he had not tasted food in ages. "You sure got done eating in a hurry, Captain."

"It's not my favorite meal."

"What? You mean the. . ." he began, then proceeded to call it by the expletive the soldiers used to describe the dish.

"I could do without the cursing, Fred," Nick said.

"Oops. Pardon me, sir. You know I'm not holy like you."

"Believe me, by myself I am not holy. But my trust in God helps make me holy. Not by anything I can do. It's by His grace alone."

Fred rolled his eyes. "Here we go on another religious ramble. Must we do this, sir?"

"Sorry, but my religious rambling does more for me than anything else. And when I get over to Europe, I'll be ready for whatever comes at me."

"Like the bullets? People get killed, you know. It could just as easily be you or me."

Nick looked at his friend with what he hoped was a challenge. "In that case, you'd better make sure you know whose side you're on and where you will end up if death does come knocking. That's why I don't need to worry about it. I know where I'm going."

"You mean in a trench with everyone else, listed as missing in action. Unless they can identify you. Then maybe you'll get to come home."

The fear from those words met Nick full force, like a breath of cold wind brushing over his soul. He refused to yield to its cruel touch. He knew there was much more to life than death. "The ground is where the old, worn-out body goes. But my spirit will be in heaven."

"You're always so sure about everything. I don't understand

it. You think you have everything all mapped out, like that climbing route where we stuck in those pitons yesterday. But you don't, Nick. You have no idea what's going to happen, nor do you really know what happens when you die. You go by some book that dictates how to run your life. But no one really knows."

Nick sensed his friend's growing animosity was wrought out of conviction. He was glad for it and even gladder there was this time to talk to Fred. They had been so busy with tasks, preparations for climbing, and a myriad of other responsibilities. He'd prayed for Fred that morning in his devotions, and it seemed God had opened a door. If only his friend would have the blinders removed from his eyes and face reality. That what Fred said was true, that death was the final chapter for those who had no hope. But there was hope after death for those who believed. Hope that ran afresh, like rivers bubbling with water from the mountain rains. Hope in eternal life.

"Actually, Fred, someone did return to tell us about death. Jesus, who rose from the dead. His disciples were eyewitnesses to His resurrection. And they knew there was more to life than just the finality of death. There's something to hold on to. Something to trust in when you go marching up a hill while the enemy is blasting away at you. To know that if a bullet does get you, there is something beyond the grave. Eternity."

"You believe in a story is all, Captain. I sure hope you see how miserable it all is out there."

"And what about you, Fred? What will happen to you when you die?"

To Nick's astonishment, Fred's face broke open into a grin. "Why, I guess I'll just turn into a grassy field for the cows to eat, won't I?" He sauntered away, whistling, to Nick's dismay. At that moment he couldn't help but feel sadness for the man. And marvel at his ignorance. If only Nick could persuade Fred to reconsider his beliefs and his choices.

Nick observed the fields before him. *Dust you are and dust you shall return.* "But there is more to this than just dust, Lord. Much more. You revealed it all in Your Word. The hope of eternal life with You. If only You could reveal it to Fred and others." He wondered then what Lucy thought of it. If God was as real to her as He was to him. How he would like to find out. And if so, it would be good to talk with someone like-minded.

He recalled how she'd mentioned God making Seneca Rocks. She had a "God consciousness," so to speak. But he knew of many, at least in the camps, who had talked about God. It was another thing to actually serve God and live one's life for God alone. Whenever the challenge came forth, and Nick proclaimed that life belonged to God, many shirked the issue or looked at him strangely. Others proudly espoused their own invincibility.

God, I can't do any of this without You. I know there are adventurers out there who don't ever acknowledge Your hand in their lives. They do things out of their own strength and belief that their lives are in their own hands. Don't they realize it can take one misstep, one slip of the rope, one thing to go wrong, and that no amount of bravado will save them in the end? They could very well meet eternity, then what will happen?

A warm breeze blew up then. The grasses waved back and forth as if God's breath signaled His favor and grace. Nick sighed. He was here for a purpose, even if a few soldiers like Fred scoffed at his faith. He would show through word and deed the reality of God, which in the end could be their saving grace.

Just then Nick heard someone call his name. Another of the sergeants marched up with the mail call. Who would be sending him a letter here, of all places? For all he knew, his parents weren't even sure of his whereabouts. Nick and his father had never been close. Dad disapproved of his adventuresome ways, wanting Nick instead to help at the family clothing store. As a youngster, the lure of the mountains had drawn Nick's heart even when he tried to learn the art of tailoring to fit eager customers with a new wardrobe. Day after day his father would shout at him to get his mind off the mountaintop and back where it belonged.

But for Nick, his mind was always on that mountain summit, and he had no plans to come down from it. He told his dad what he wanted to do with his life. Angry words followed. His father then turned to Nick's younger brother, Phil, who was a natural at the business side of things. For himself, Nick took off for the mountains and never looked back. As far as he knew, no one had told them about this trip to West Virginia. He decided that when he returned to Colorado he should at least let his mother know what was happening, especially before the army sent him anywhere else. She always worried for his safety. And he knew she prayed for him.

Nick stared at the unfamiliar handwriting spelling out his name and the camp of Seneca Rocks. He liked the cursive writing. Large and flowery, as if the person was cheerful at heart. Ripping it open, he unfolded the paper to find a message from Lucy Bland. It was short, simple, and kind. He tucked it into the pocket of his shirt. He should write her back tonight if he didn't forget. Tell her how much he enjoyed their visits. Ask her when she would come by with more fresh muffins. In response, his stomach complained from the lack of dinner. Striding back toward camp, he touched the letter over his chest. Dear little Lucy. She wasn't little, by no means. She was a robust, grown woman with eyes of fire, eager to help him with anything. If only he knew what to do. Surely he couldn't handle a relationship right now. That was out of the question. But a friendship would work. A person could always use friends. Especially when his own friendship with Fred teetered on the brink of dissolution. Lucy would fit the bill nicely.

ã

The next day Nick called for a meeting with Fred. "What's up?" Fred asked.

"We're going to take a few of the experienced men out and test climb the route."

"Sure thing, Nick ol' boy. I'm ready to get going."

"Good. And another thing. You will address me as Captain Landers. One more infraction like that and I'll have to write you up. This is serious business, and we must conduct ourselves properly. Do you understand, Sergeant?"

Fred whirled, his eyes wide, his mouth gaping in astonishment. He appeared ready to issue a rebuke but wisely clamped his lips shut.

Nick rattled off the names of the men he wanted to accompany them—several privates who had previous climbing experience. "Fall in," Nick ordered when the men arrived. They stood in a single line of formation, their eyes focused straight ahead. "We're going to do a test climb of the main pitch today. You're the best we have, so I know you'll do what is expected of you. In turn, you will instruct the others on proper climbing protocol."

"What exactly are we climbing, sir?"

Nick pointed to the crest of rocks reaching toward the sky. "That. Seneca Rocks."

The men observed the rocks with curiosity and trepidation. One or two murmured their anxiety while the majority nodded, their facial expressions as stony as the rocks, determined to meet whatever challenge was thrown at them. Nick recalled a time not long ago when he'd stood before a commanding officer with an eagerness to prove himself and did so with determination. He hoped the men would have the same determination to succeed, and afterward, he would lead them to victory on future hillsides yet to be determined.

Fred returned and stood by the privates. He looked off into the distance, refusing to meet Nick's eye. With coils of rope over each shoulder, carabiners clinking, Nick led the group through the grassy fields toward the rocky faces. He tried not to think about Fred, who brought up the rear of the group, though his anger was palpable. Nick sighed. If only things weren't so complicated in life. He wanted to maintain order and discipline, but he also needed companionship and the camaraderie of a friend. Then with Lucy thrown into all this, it had become an entangled web of mixed feelings, to say the least.

Nick sighed. For now he couldn't worry about it. He had a job to do. He must devote his energy to the route they would face today, an easy three-pitch climb that he and Fred had laid out with pitons yesterday. He'd done the lead climbing to hammer in the pitons while Fred held the safety rope and belayed him. He was glad he and Fred hadn't had a falling-out then or he might have been a bit concerned with Fred on the other end of the rope. But Fred had always been there, no matter what. Like during that blizzard in the Rockies and when they did other training exercises. Nick did not doubt the man's abilities or willingness to keep him safe.

Suddenly Nick heard what sounded like a youngster crying. He took off toward the base of the cliff where a young boy stood. The boy's face was wet with tears. "What's the matter, young fellow? Are you hurt?"

"It's Carl," the boy said, pointing up at the jagged rocks. "He's stuck up there and can't get down. What are we gonna do? He'll die!"

Nick squinted to see another boy hovering near a rocky precipice nearly sixty feet up. "Carl!" he shouted. "Can you hear me?"

"I—I can't get down," a tremulous voice answered. "Help me. I—I don't know what to do. I think I'm gonna fall!"

"Just stay calm. Keep away from the ledge. Is there a bush or tree near you?"

"Y—yes. A couple of those stubby trees."

"Okay. Now, Carl, I want you to go ahead and grab hold of one of the trees and stay put. Don't let go for any reason until I come and get you. Okay?" Nick paused for a moment to listen, even as his heart began to race.

"O—okay," came the faint voice. "I found a tree."

By this time the other men had arrived, breathless from following Nick's lead through the dense underbrush to the base of the rocks. "What's that young boy doing way up there?" Fred exclaimed, shielding his eyes from the glare of the sun off the rocky face.

"I don't know how he got up there, but we have to get him down. I'm going to have to lay in pitons, Fred, just like yesterday. You okay with belaying?"

"Of course, Captain."

Nick stared into his friend's face, knowing he could trust Fred even if they had a difference of opinion on other matters. "I'll have to carry up another hundred feet of rope."

"You up to this?" Fred asked.

"It's good training. And good for the other men, as well." Nick tied himself in with the rope to form a harness. He attached extra pitons on a sling and tucked in a hammer to pound them in with.

"Take a drink." Fred offered him his canteen. Nick took a healthy swallow while assessing the task that lay before him. Handing the canteen back to Fred, he positioned himself. "Okay, Carl, I'm climbing up to get you," he shouted. "Are you hanging on to that tree like I told you?"

"Y–yeah. Hurry!"

"Okay. Don't let go, no matter what." Turning to Fred he called out, "On belay?"

"Belay on," Fred told him, the rope secured around his own waist but slack in his hands.

"Climbing." Nick began the perilous ascent, looking for hand- and footholds. When he came to a healthy crack in the rock, he pounded in a piton with a piton hammer, fastened a carabiner to it, and connected his rope.

"Climb on," Fred reassured him from below.

Sweat poured off Nick's face. How he wished he could enjoy the climb, thinking of the beauty of the valley unfolding below him. But all he could think about was that young boy and how close to death he had come. Whatever possessed him to climb this far on his own? Nick hammered in five more pitons until he reached the ledge. There, clinging to a stubby tree, was a boy about twelve or thirteen, shaking like a branch caught in a stiff wind. The boy suddenly let go and came toward Nick.

"No, stay where you are. Hang on to that tree. I'm going to fasten the rope to it." When Nick had the rope anchored, he called down to Fred. "Off belay! Give me some slack." Then turning to Carl, he said, "Okay, Carl, I'm going to tie this other rope around you, and we're going to lower you to the ground. It's not really like rappelling, but it will give you a little taste of it. Want to try?"

"I—I guess. I just want to get down from here. I didn't know I wouldn't be able to get down."

Nick secured one end of the rope to Carl's skinny waist, the other end to the tree. He made a figure eight in the rope a few feet from the tree and, using a carabiner, attached the rope to his harness for stability. "Okay, I'm going to let you down nice and easy. It will be like walking down the side of a rock wall. Just use your feet and pretend like you can walk down it. Okay?"

"Okay."

With a prayer on his lips, Nick slowly began to lower Carl toward Fred's position. The boy took small steps against the rock wall, bouncing as he did while Nick guided the rope. When he heard an exclamation from below, Nick breathed a sigh of relief and thanked God for His hand of protection. He then checked the anchor of the rope tied off on the tree and rappelled down to where the two boys stood.

"Whew, I'm glad you're safe," he said to Carl, wiping the sweat from his face before taking up Fred's canteen. "Whatever gave you the idea of going up there without safety equipment?"

"I don't know, sir. It looked really easy to me. And. . .I wanted to do what you do."

Nick sighed, looking at the boys. It dawned on him then who they were, now that the rescue had been complete. They were none other than Lucy's brothers, the same ones he had met in the field the other day. "I'm glad you two boys are safe, but now I need to get you back to where you belong. The Bland household, right?"

"Yeah, but we can find our own way back home," Carl said, scooting away from Nick's grasp.

Nick took hold of his shirtsleeve. "Not so fast. I intend to take you there myself." To Fred he said, "Think you all can manage the climb? Might as well do this section for starters."

Fred saluted. "We've got a handle on it, Captain. See you back at camp."

Nick stepped aside and whispered, "Thanks for your help, Fred. I appreciate it."

The man gave him the semblance of a smile before redirecting his attention to the other soldiers and began shouting orders.

Nick's gaze diverted to Carl and Tim, who looked more scared now than when he'd first arrived at the rocks. "Okay, boys. Let's get you home."

"Really, sir, we know the way," Carl protested. "Don't you have other things to do?"

"Plenty. But after a situation like this, I need your parents to know what happened and to make sure you don't do anything like that again. You were blessed this time. Next time you may not be. Rock climbing can be deadly if you don't know what you're doing. And even people who do know have been killed by a piton breaking loose, a rope giving way, or slipping on the rocks. This kind of climbing can never be taken lightly."

Carl stared at the ground, scuffing up the grass with his

shoes. "Daddy won't let me out of the house if you tell on me," he mumbled. "Just tell him we got lost or something. Please?"

"Is that being honest?"

"It beats getting a whipping."

"Well, maybe a whipping isn't such a bad idea, considering what could have happened to the both of you. Like getting yourselves killed. C'mon." Nick moved swiftly through the fields with the two boys dragging their feet. How glad he was that everything worked out all right for the Bland boys.

Just then he remembered a comment Fred uttered the day they first encountered the boys in the pasture.

"It seems to me, my dear Captain, that you are linked to this Bland family in more ways than one. There's just no escaping them."

Truer now than ever, Lord, Nick added silently. *But I have to wonder where all this will lead in the end.*

eight

Lucy looked in the oven at the dish she'd prepared—chicken and dumplings, her father's favorite. Daddy was coming home for the noon meal, a rarity as the lumber mill often kept him away for hours on end, sometimes late into the evening. But with his expected arrival today at noon, Momma had decided to have the main meal then so he could enjoy it before his business took him away again. Lucy promptly set to work making the dish as soon as her mother informed her of the plan.

She now took the casserole out of the oven to find it nicely browned, the gravy bubbling through the cracker crust, when a commotion erupted in the front yard. "Must be Carl and Tim," she told Momma, untying her apron. "They can smell cooking a mile away."

She came to the window, prepared to see them racing each other to the porch, flinging open the screen door, waving their soiled hands in her face while their voices begged for food. Instead, to her amazement, she saw Nick enter the yard, leading each boy by the arm. Both brothers had flushed and downcast faces. Neither said a word. She opened the screen door. "Captain Landers, what happened?"

"Are your folks at home, Lucy?"

She stepped aside as Momma came to the door.

"What's this about? Carl, Tim, where have you been?"

"It wasn't anything," Carl began.

91

"You sure about that?" Nick said, nudging him slightly.

"I just wanted to try it out. It wasn't anything."

Nick frowned. "Getting stranded on a ledge sixty feet up with no safety equipment and no way down is hardly nothing. And especially when others had to stop their own business to come up there and rescue you."

"Oh, no!" Momma cried, just as Daddy walked into the room. "Did you hear what happened, Dick? Carl and Tim were up there on Seneca Rocks and this soldier had to rescue them."

"What's this?" Daddy came forward, the morning paper in his hand. Nick quickly unfolded the details. "I don't believe it. The one day I get off at noon and you boys have to do something like this."

"I didn't get stuck up there," Tim declared. "Carl did."

"You could've been hurt!" Momma wailed.

"Killed is more like it," Daddy said in a matter-of-fact tone that sent another wail from Momma's lips. "We're very thankful, Mister. . ."

"Landers, sir. Captain Nick Landers with the Mountain Training Group."

"Thank you, Captain Landers. I'm much obliged. Now surely you can come in and share the noon meal with us. It's the least we can do to thank you."

Lucy's heart nearly skipped a beat as she watched Nick look beyond her father to the table in the dining room and the dish of chicken and dumplings, its steamy aroma wafting through the house. "Well. . .I do have things to do, but I left my sergeant in charge. I suppose he can handle it."

"Good. Come on in then, and make yourself at home."

Lucy thought she had died and gone to heaven. The man

she dreamed of day and night now stood in the foyer of her humble home. His gaze settled on her for a brief moment before taking in the sights of the home. "The washroom is over there if you want to clean up," she said, pointing the way.

"Thanks." He whistled a tune Lucy didn't recognize. He washed and then tried to scoop up a mound of his dark hair and comb it back with his fingers. "Here's a comb," she added from the hallway, offering him one of her father's old ones.

He seemed startled, then took it. "Thanks." In several swift strokes he had his hair neatly parted to one side and combed back.

"Sorry my brothers gave you such a headache today," she said when he stepped out of the washroom.

"Backache is more like it. I think I pulled something on the last part of that pitch."

He followed her to the table where the two boys stared down at their plates in silence, refusing to acknowledge anyone. Lucy nearly chuckled when she saw the guilt written on both their faces, especially on the outspoken Carl. It was rare to see him so silent. No doubt Daddy's presence fueled their despondency as he glared at the two boys from the head of the table.

"I'd send them to their rooms," Daddy said, "but I don't like hungry boys under my roof. I think there are other punishments better than an empty belly, don't you think, Captain Landers?"

"Please call me Nick, sir. And yes, I'm sure there are. In fact, locking oneself away in a room for a time to think things through can be a good idea."

Daddy offered a prayer for the meal, then served Nick a huge mound of chicken and dumplings. "I think Captain Landers has made a good suggestion, boys. After your chores are done, you will go to your room and think about what you did today."

The boys said nothing but picked at their food.

"I remember being in their shoes when I was their age," Nick added. "I loved the mountains. One time I got lost up there and hadn't come home by dinnertime. My mother was frantic. When Dad finally did find me, he sent me to my room for a week."

"A whole week!" Carl said in alarm. "Why a week?"

"'Cause I could've been hurt badly. It made me think real hard about what I had done. They let me out for meals, of course. And the chores. But it did me good. I think about that time often when I'm mountaineering, to make sure I'm always careful and not to glorify myself in what I do. It's good to be humbled once in a while. Pride comes before the fall, you know, and you don't want to be caught falling off some cliff. It's a long way down."

Lucy said nothing but quietly enjoyed listening to Nick's conversation. He ate the food she'd prepared as if savoring a gourmet meal. She imagined herself as his wife then, preparing the evening meal, making sure he had a comb ready to do up his hair. She'd even wash and iron his clothes if he'd let her. Anything, so long as she could relish the time spent with him and become a part of his world, a world that still seemed so far away.

"This is excellent," Nick said, helping himself to another portion. "I'll have to say I haven't been able to eat much of the camp food recently. Hopefully that will be changing as some of the good folks around here bring supplies to the camp."

"What do you eat?" Carl wondered, his mouth full of biscuit.

"Oh, stews and soups mostly. We had chipped beef on bread the other day."

"Yum."

Nick chuckled. "You wouldn't have said 'yum' to this, I'll tell you. More like *ugh*. That is unless you enjoy salty strips mixed with paste—the cook's attempt at making it resemble chipped beef in gravy." He hesitated. "I suppose I shouldn't be complaining about the food. There are plenty of people in other places who have nothing."

"Why not?" Daddy said. "You have every right to complain. They ought to be feeding you men the best food there is, with the sacrifices you're making."

"They're probably trying to save money for the war effort," Momma added, passing the chicken and dumplings to Nick.

"That is no excuse. Of course, I'm no cook, Captain Landers. Now Lucy here, her mother taught her well. She makes the best food. In fact, she made this meal today."

Again Nick's gaze fell on her and lingered there for a time, as if appreciating this tidbit of news. He then dished up his third helping and took a fourth biscuit. He winked in her direction as if to say he loved her cooking. She felt warmth rise in her cheeks and a sudden shyness. If only she could meet his steady gaze with one of her own, one she hoped would reveal her innermost heart. Instead she felt like a schoolgirl on the playground, her feet scuffing up dirt, wondering what to say to the most popular boy in the class.

"She's a great cook," Nick agreed. "She made me the best blueberry muffins."

"Really," Daddy said. "So you two have already met?"

Oh, no, Lucy thought. At once her shyness was replaced by decisiveness. "Well, I thought it was a nice gesture, Daddy, seeing as what kind of food the men have to put up with at that camp."

"Your daughter was kind enough to also show my sergeant and me the way to the base of the rocks for our climbing maneuvers," Nick added. "If it hadn't been for her help, we might have spent valuable time wandering around and not had the opportunity to promptly begin the training. It's these acts of kindness that help us accomplish what we need to do."

Daddy nodded. Lucy caught the slight smile on Nick's face, as if he were trying to soothe her nerves.

"We all need to do our part in this effort," Daddy said. "Bring out the tea, Jane, will you? I'm sure the captain here would like a good cup of hot tea."

Nick wiped his mouth with his napkin. "Well, I must say, that was a great dinner. Best I've had in years." Again came his smile of appreciation in Lucy's direction. How she would love to pull him aside for a chat on the front porch. Instead he stood to his feet and dropped his napkin on the table. "I hate to eat and run, but I left my contingent of men by the rocks. I should go check on them."

"So where are you staying, Captain Landers?" Daddy asked. "I hear there are officers staying in Elkins. Pretty nice accommodations, as well."

"I'm staying in the tent barracks by Seneca Rocks, sir."

Daddy took a swig of tea, sat back, and shook his head. "That's no place for men like you with your kind of responsibility. We need to do what's right to keep our officers healthy. We have a spare bedroom here. You're welcome to stay with us. We're just down the road from the camp, so you'd be pretty much near your men if the need arises. And I'm sure your sergeants can help, as well."

Lucy thought she might collapse if not for sitting in a chair. Her heart began to take off like a mare racing across the field. *This can't be happening.* Daddy had actually invited Nick Landers to dwell under their roof? Was this heaven sent? God's answer to all her questioning of late?

"That's thoughtful of you, sir, but I wouldn't want to impose."

"It's no imposition. I'm sure we can learn a lot about what's happening. It would do the boys some good to have a soldier here to keep them in line. Eh, Carl and Tim?"

The boys stared at him with wide eyes. "Well, I'm not so sure," Carl began.

Daddy laughed. "You see? I believe it's settled, that is, if you agree, Captain Landers."

"I would be a fool to say no, sir, seeing as my tent did leak in the rainstorm last week."

"Good. Then we will expect you for dinner unless you want more of that food you were describing. Unfortunately, I won't be here some evenings, but I know the missus and Lucy will make you feel at home."

"Thank you again for your kind offer and for the delicious meal." Nick shook Daddy's hand and then began making his way to the front door.

Lucy slipped out of the dining room and followed Nick to the porch. "I guess we'll see you later," she said, hoping she didn't sound too eager. She didn't want to chase him away him because of some obsession. She wanted their relationship to be real, to mature naturally, in God's perfect timing.

"Yes. And thanks for the great meal. You're quite a cook." He nodded, offered her another dazzling smile, and headed for the road. Lucy did her best to contain the happiness welling up within her. This couldn't have been planned any better if she'd tried. "I just need to let it go and let God take control," she murmured.

Just then she caught sight of Carl making his way to the stairs and his room. "Carl, you're the best!" Lucy called up to him.

"What?"

"For getting yourself trapped on that cliff. If that hadn't happened, Captain Landers would never have come here. And now he's our houseguest. I owe it all to you."

"Goodie, goodie for you," Carl muttered, climbing the stairs one by one.

It's more than good. It's a blessing. And maybe I'll find out all that I need to know, especially about the man who has conquered my heart. Thank You, God! She raced back outside to the porch, hoping to catch one last glimpse of Nick walking down the road, heading for the camp. He had since vanished, but she knew he would return tonight. And she would make plans for a wonderful welcome-to-our-home meal, complete with plenty of biscuits. There may even be time for conversation afterward, perhaps during a moonlit walk. Lucy leaned against the porch railing. Everything was slowly coming together and before the meeting with Allen on Friday. She still wasn't sure how she would talk herself out of the date they had agreed on. Maybe honesty was the way she should go. Be forthright and tell him about Nick.

Tell Allen what? That I'm in love with Nick, but I still don't know how he feels about me? That I could be imagining some relationship and then be left out in the cold when he leaves with his troops? That Allen could be angry with me forever and others gossiping around town, wondering what I'm doing? Lucy straightened. She would take everything as it came. And right now, she planned to make Nick Landers feel so welcome, he would never want to leave her side.

nine

Friday came, and with it, nervous jitters as Lucy waited all day for Allen to stop by the house and ask about their planned date in Petersburg. She'd stayed up most of the night, rehearsing what she would say when the time came. Since that day when she talked to Allen at the store, Lucy had not seen hide nor hair of him. She wasn't sure what to make of it. Maybe Carl had gotten a hold of him and told him right off that Nick was their houseguest. At times she considered moseying on down to the store to see what was afoot. After all, this not knowing was driving her crazy. Not that she wanted a date with Allen or have him push her into a corner she couldn't get out of. But she did want to know his intentions and if they could at least remain friends.

Momma glanced into the room just as Lucy was finishing the speech she might need to give later. Momma stared with a quizzical look before shaking her head. "Really, Lucy. Will you never get your head out of the clouds? Ever since those soldiers came, I don't know what's come over you."

"I'm fine, Momma. I was wondering. . .has anyone—have you heard or seen any messages or anyone stop by asking for me?"

"Should I have?"

"Allen said something about getting together today, but I haven't heard from him all week."

Was it just her imagination or did her mother's face brighten? Lucy never knew Momma cared that much for Allen. Though that time Allen brought her home and she left him standing on the porch, Momma had come to his defense. She hoped Momma and Daddy weren't assuming that she'd marry the man. Other things were at work right now. Like Nick Landers, who gave her a quick good-bye that morning after drinking down a cup of coffee and eating three crullers Lucy had fried up the night before.

"No, I haven't heard any news about Allen. I did see him heading out of town on Wednesday. Maybe something came up."

"He didn't say he was going out of town."

Momma stood in the doorway, her arms folded. "I just wonder if he's up to something. Sneaking off without telling anyone doesn't seem like the Allen I know. Maybe he's getting ready for something big."

Lucy didn't want to dive into speculations right now, even if Momma hinted at them. She prayed silently that Allen wasn't going off to buy an engagement ring. She couldn't bear the thought of confronting him while he stood there with a gift box in hand and a look of expectation on his face.

"I'm sure there's a good reason," Lucy said quickly, spinning about to avoid seeing Momma's questioning expression. How she wished she could confide in Momma about her feelings for Nick, but she didn't really know what her mother thought of the handsome soldier. Momma had said little since Nick arrived, even if Daddy peppered the man with questions about the war effort and the soldiers he trained. In turn, Nick entertained them with his experiences in leading the men on the rocks and his adventures in Colorado.

When Momma disappeared, Lucy contemplated a new set of worries. If Allen was indeed planning a marriage proposal, she would have to act soon. But first she must know Nick's intentions. As far as she knew, he had no romantic inclinations. His contact with her had only been congenial at best. Lucy blew out a sigh that ruffled her bangs. If only she could corner him, maybe on some moonlit road, and find out what he wanted for the future besides adventure. If he ever thought of finding a woman special enough to marry. Or if he had someone special back in Colorado. Then she might have a better idea what to do about Allen.

"I'm going to the store, Lucy!" Momma called up the stairs. "Be back soon."

Oh no, she thought, rushing to the window as Momma headed down the porch steps. She bit her lip. What if Momma told Mr. Hopper what she'd said about Allen? That nonsense about expecting a date tonight? Lucy sighed in exasperation. If only she hadn't found herself lost in some dark alley of confusion with two men mixed up in it. If only these men would make up their minds the way she wanted.

Lucy, when have you taken the time to ask God about His *way? What* He *wants for your life? Not your will, but* His *will be done.* Again she bit her lip. What if God wanted her to be with Allen? Could she accept it? Could she say good-bye to Nick? If so, then why had He opened the door for Nick to come and live under their roof—providing a situation that only added to the attraction she felt for him in her heart? Surely God wouldn't do this unless there was some plan.

Lucy tried to busy herself with mundane activities while waiting for her mother's return. When she finally heard the front door close, she stepped out into the foyer, pushing strands of hair behind one ear. "How was your errand?"

"You can help me with this," Momma said, handing her a

paper bag full of groceries. "Having another hungry man in the house sure makes the food go fast."

"Nick told me he tried to give Daddy money for his room and board, but Daddy refused."

"It's just our way of helping the cause," Momma said. "With your brothers too young to enlist, I guess your father felt this was one small way we could help."

"I'm sure you're glad that Carl and Tim are too young," Lucy remarked.

"Some days I am very glad. Other days, especially when they find themselves in a whirl of mischief, I think having them in the army might do them some good. Though having Captain Landers under our roof has seemed to put them on their best behavior. It's good to have another man here, especially with your father working late at the mill on odd days. I feel more secure, too."

Lucy took out the packages of flour and sugar to stow away in the cupboard. "Any other news?" she hedged.

"Leslie Watson had her baby. Mrs. Sampson has something wrong with her heart, or so she says. Others are moaning about the soldiers that are everywhere. I had one man ask me why we are keeping a soldier under our roof. I asked him what he's doing to help the cause." Momma chuckled. "Guess I can speak my mind when I need to." She paused. "And speaking of that, I asked Mr. Hopper about Allen. It seems Allen had to go out of town unexpectedly. His grandfather on his mother's side has taken ill. You remember him, I'm sure, the one who lives in Charleston."

"Yes, I remember him." Lucy recalled the older gentleman who'd stayed for several years when she and Allen were young. Allen was named after his grandfather and they were close.

He called him Grandpa Al and they would often go fishing together in the North Fork River. "I hope he's all right."

Momma shook her head. "Not from what Ed says. They don't think he will live much longer, which is why Allen left to go visit him. No sense in seeing someone after they're dead. You should see them when they're alive so you can say your good-byes."

For some reason the statement saddened Lucy. She had only thought of life, after all, here by Seneca Rocks, watching soldiers like Nick train and carry on with their duties. It hadn't truly dawned on her until now that those men trained to go into the heat of battle. And battles meant death. Many of them might never return. She shuddered and turned away.

"I didn't mean to upset you, Lucy. I know how you all used to do things together when his grandfather came to visit."

"Yes," she said absently, still thinking of Nick. What would she do if the army called him away to that dreadful war in Europe? Was it right for her to marry someone like Nick, only to see their love die on some distant battlefield? How could she bear being a widow? Her throat began to close over at the thought, making her choke with emotion.

"I'm sorry." Momma came and wrapped her arm around Lucy. "I know it must be hard."

Lucy wanted to confide in her mother that while she was sorry for Allen's grandfather, it was Nick and their future that left her choked up with worry. Nick wounded or lost or even killed. Life without Nick by her side. Perhaps these were the birth pangs of true love.

"I'll make some tea," Momma offered. "We can sit on the porch and say a prayer for his recovery."

Lucy said nothing as she fetched two teacups and the tea

strainer while Momma put the kettle on to boil. If only she had the courage to express her thoughts. If only there were someone to talk to about her feelings. After the kettle sang, Momma poured the steaming water into cups.

"This is nice," she said with a smile, carrying out the tea. Lucy followed with a small plate of crullers left over from breakfast. "We should do this more often, but there's always things to do, it seems. Now with that soldier around here, everything is so hectic."

"You don't sound as if you like Nick that much, Momma," Lucy noted carefully.

"On the contrary, he's a very nice man. And, of course, he rescued Carl and Tim from the rocks. Like I said before, those boys have been angels with him around." Momma sipped her tea while Lucy stared into hers, watching the tiny fragments of tea leaves chase each other around. "Come, let's say a prayer for Allen's granddad."

Lucy obediently set her cup down and closed her eyes. Not only did she pray for the elderly man but also for Nick, that his day would go well and that he would come home in a jovial mood, setting her heart at ease. That she would know beyond a shadow of a doubt whether they had a future together.

"Amen," Momma said. "I'm sure he will feel better soon. The Lord has answered my prayers so many times. Just as I've prayed for you, Lucy."

Lucy looked at her mother curiously. "What have you prayed for?"

"Oh, many things. Mostly that you will find a nice man to marry. And I think soon you may get your wish."

Lucy returned her gaze to the cup. "Why do you say that?"

"Oh, just a feeling. Mother's intuition, I suppose. I think you will make someone a fine wife, Lucy."

She opened her mouth, ready to inform her mother how she would love to be a certain army captain's wife and live with him in Colorado, but she could not speak the words. Instead she finished her tea and told Momma she was going for a walk. Momma said nothing, though Lucy could tell her sudden withdrawal had surprised her mother. She wished everything could be spelled out clearly, but matters of the heart were the most difficult to discuss. Especially when one's heart wasn't sure which way to turn on the path of life.

❧

That evening Lucy waited anxiously for Nick's return. In a way she looked forward to seeing him again, but in another way, she felt shy and reserved, especially considering her thoughts of late. If she weren't so nervous, she might be tempted to come right out and ask Nick if he had feelings for her. If he had any notion of a relationship or even marriage or if she should accept the proposal she was sure Allen had waiting for her upon his return. But the thoughts stayed buried. She knew she couldn't bring herself to ask Nick such personal, forward questions. It must come naturally from the heart, something that God birthed within the both of them. Maybe tonight there would be some glimpse into the inner workings of Nick's heart. Something that would guide her decision-making and spark hope for the future.

Nick arrived late that evening, much to her dismay. Dinner was already on the table, being enjoyed by the family, when he came trudging in. Lucy listened to him enter the foyer, moan, and retreat out the door. She excused herself to see what the trouble was. She found him outside, trying to remove his mud-caked boots. Chunks of mud lay scattered on the wooden floor of the foyer. She fetched the broom as she heard him fumbling outside on the porch, knocking mud off of his boots. The door opened and suddenly she and Nick collided.

"Oops, I'm sorry." He stepped back when he saw her standing there with the broom. "You don't need to clean up after me. I can do it. I forgot to take off my boots."

"It's nothing."

"I figured I'm probably too late for dinner. Sorry about that. I would be happy with a sandwich or something."

"You're not too late. Though you'd better get in there before Carl and Tim eat it all."

He walked past her, stopped, and turned. "Are you coming, too, or did you eat already?"

She looked up, surprised at his concern. At this point she was willing to take any inkling of concern for her well-being as a sign of hope. "I had a little, but I'm not that hungry tonight."

He stood there, silent for a moment, then walked into the dining room where Lucy heard the greetings, including Daddy's welcome. Daddy took great pleasure in having the officer under his roof. He seemed to radiate with pride, as if his hospitality would earn him a medal. No doubt Daddy also liked bragging to his coworkers about his contribution to the war effort by housing one of the higher-ups. Lucy couldn't care less about such things. She only wanted to know which man she should marry.

When Lucy finished her duty, she entered the dining room to see Nick with a heap of stew on his plate. Carl was asking questions about the day's activities. Nick looked right at home among her family. He smiled and chatted as if he had known them for years. He would make a wonderful son-in-law and brother-in-law. Perfect to keep her unruly brothers in line and for Daddy who enjoyed his presence. And Momma would go along with whatever Daddy said. It all seemed so right. But one thing was lacking. A commitment on Nick's part. A sense of adoration. The knowledge that he loved her.

"A great meal once again," Nick said with satisfaction as Momma placed a cup of tea before him. "I do hope, though, you will allow me to at least offer a bit of support toward my room and board."

"I won't hear of it," Daddy told him. "We're just glad we can help. So long as you are able to do your job, training those boys of yours."

"It is a job, that's for sure," he agreed. "Especially trying to get them to do what I want. Many of them are scared, and I guess rightly so. It takes a lot of calm words and prayer to get some of them to even put one foot in a foothold on the rock and to trust that the ropes won't give way. But I like to think how it compares to our walk of faith. It takes faith to trust God with the things in our lives. Things that seem too difficult, hoping He won't let us fall. I think more than anything else, I'm learning about God and His Word as I instruct."

Lucy marveled. Nick was so much more spiritual than Allen. Allen went to church, yes. He did pray sometimes. But he hardly mentioned God in his conversations. Nick talked about the Lord as if He were his closest companion, there for him always, a Friend in times of need. Nick trusted God with everything.

When the family retired to the living room to hear the

evening radio programs, Lucy began clearing the table. Suddenly she saw Nick's beefy hands reach out to pick up a few bowls. "No sense leaving you with all this to clean up," he said.

"Oh, it's no bother. I'm used to it."

He stood there holding the bowls, appearing thoughtful. "Is something bothering you, Lucy?"

Caught off guard by his question, she trembled. "Why do you say that?"

"I don't know, but ever since I came here, you seem kind of put out. Like my presence bothers you or something."

"Of course not," she said, trying to look relaxed even as her voice shook when she said the words.

"I don't want you to feel that way. I hope I'm not making more work for you."

"Of course not. I guess I have a lot on my mind these days."

He nodded as if he understood, though she couldn't figure out how he would know what was on her mind. He continued to help clear the table and then armed himself with a towel while she proceeded to wash the dishes. "You don't need to do this," she said again.

"Believe me, this is a nice change from what I do every day. Being with a bunch of rough, gritty soldiers can get to you. And they certainly don't smell as nice as you do."

Lucy felt her cheeks heat up. "I know after Daddy and the boys come in from work, they do tend to smell like the great outdoors. But so do I, after I come in from the garden."

"I don't know, but there's something about women. They never smell bad." He laughed. "Not sure why I'm on that topic. Like I go sniffing around or something, which I don't."

Lucy chuckled in spite of herself. "I'm sure a nice man like you has a girlfriend, though. Maybe in Colorado?"

"Used to. She hated my mountaineering. But it seems your boyfriend likes the mountains."

Again her cheeks flamed. "Allen is just a friend. We've known each other since we were children. That's all."

Nick said little else. After the dishes were done, he joined the family in the sitting room where they sat listening to the radio. Lucy stood in the doorway watching him amid her family. How well he fit in—as if he were meant to be there. His gaze then met hers. She stepped back into the hallway, suddenly embarrassed. What would he think of her staring at him? Maybe it was time he knew how she felt. Maybe she could bring out that first letter she wrote and slip it under his pillow while he was away at camp. Or tuck it into his shirt pocket as he slept; the pocket that sat directly over his heart. He would find it the next day and the words would seal their future. If only the time were now.

ten

"That's it for today, men," Nick announced when the last of the team had safely rappelled to firm ground. A round of cheers rose up from the group. Some slapped each other on the back, congratulating each other on a job well done. One young man, still trembling from the encounter with the rocks that day, could only peel off his helmet, wipe the perspiration dribbling down his face, and claim he was glad the day was finished.

"Sure hope I don't have to do that again," he murmured. "Once is enough for me."

"Sorry to be the bearer of bad news, but we'll be doing it again tomorrow," Nick reminded them. "So don't relax too much. Just remember all we've done. The next time it will be as easy as pie."

The men laughed except for the nervous private. They talked with one another about their adventure as they made their way back to camp. Nick watched Fred silently gather up the equipment. Since their falling out, Fred had said little to Nick. At times Nick regretted the harsh tone he had used with his friend, especially threatening to report him for disregarding the use of titles. But Nick knew he had to maintain clear authority. The young GIs would respect him if the chain of command remained intact. So far it had worked well, but he wondered if it had been worth sacrificing the only true friend he had in the entire outfit.

"So how do you think the day went, Sergeant Watkins?" Nick asked.

Fred glanced up, his eyes wide. "You talking to me, Captain?"

"There's no one else here by that name. I noticed you haven't said hardly a word to me for days."

Fred heaved a coil of rope over his shoulder. "Just trying not to say the wrong thing so I don't get written up, sir."

Nick paused. "What if I said, since the men are gone, that you can have a personal 'at ease' during our conversation?"

"I'd say that once I get going, I probably would never end it at the appropriate time. And I might get into trouble with my CO, which I don't want to do."

Nick frowned as his friend began the slow trek back toward camp. At that instant he felt entirely alone. Despite their ranks and their differences, Fred was still his friend. They had been through the good and the ugly together, working first in the mountains of Colorado and now undertaking this mission. Nick enjoyed the talks they had when they sat up nights, trying to figure out what to do with the men. But ever since the training program began, there had been no such talks. There was no one to confide in but God. Not that there was anything wrong with that, but Nick missed the human interaction. The friendship.

He took up his backpack and helmet and hurried to join Fred. "Hey, Fred, if I could get you a dinner invitation, would you be interested?"

"What? I like the food served in camp, Captain. I'm not picky like some soldiers who will remain nameless."

Nick had to chuckle. "Quite true, and yes, I'm picky. But what if I said I know someone who's serving up a good smoked ham tonight? And biscuits that melt in your mouth. Could you be enticed to come?"

Fred stopped in his tracks. He tipped up his helmet and glanced at Nick. "What are you trying to do, Captain?"

"I'm trying to accomplish what I need to succeed, Sergeant. I wanted us to be a team by preserving the chain of command when we are with the other men. But at the same time, I could also use a friend."

"Like I said, you should have gone with the other COs to Elkins. Instead you take up at that mountain dame's home to be with her and her kid brothers. You're never around here anymore. I end up having to play cards with a bunch of privates who don't know a club from a spade."

"Let's just say that my association with the family can now get you a good meal. You even complained about the 'baby food' they serve here. So how about it?"

Fred's face erupted into a grin. "You know I'd be a fool to refuse a ham dinner, Captain Landers."

"Good. If you don't mind then, I'm going to make your presence known to the family before you get there. You know the house, the same one we visited when we first arrived, the white one with the porch."

"I know it. Hope they tie up that dog of theirs."

"They have been, so don't worry. Come around seven."

"Seven." He adjusted the rope he carried. "And thanks for thinking of me, Captain." Fred trudged on, but Nick saw those steps leading them back to the path they had once trod together, the path of friendship that he needed more and more. Even if they were different men with different ranks, and yes, different beliefs, they were friends for a reason. And Nick would preserve that friendship to the best of his ability. Now as he looked back toward the Blands' home, he hoped Lucy would agree to the plan.

⁂

"You sure were right about the food, Captain Landers," Fred said with a sigh, patting his stomach. "That was the best meal I've had since I entered the army. Years, in fact. It was excellent."

Nick glanced across the table and saw the slow flush of appreciation highlight Lucy's cheeks. He never saw anyone looking prettier. She then stood to her feet to perform her customary duty of clearing the dishes. Nick flew to his feet, as well. "Allow me," he said, taking the plates from her hand. "You've done plenty tonight." He ignored the looks circulating around the table, from Fred to Lucy's parents, then to the boys, who poked each other in glee. He didn't care what they thought. This young woman did more than anyone. He sensed her silence the last few days was because of the ceaseless chores. Though he disliked the idea of making more work by having Fred join in, he needed to reestablish a rapport with the man. Maybe once the dishes were done he could take Lucy aside and explain why he'd invited Fred—that she was helping a good cause by reaching out to a man whose heart was as far away from God as a heart could be.

Mrs. Bland brought out her rose print teapot and cups for the evening round of tea. When Nick finished drying the dishes, he took his seat opposite Fred and asked for the sugar bowl.

"It's going well, sir," Fred was saying to a question posed by Mr. Bland. "Of course, you get some boys who can't seem to remember when's the last time they climbed a haystack. I mean, we all were climbers way back when. I'm sure your two boys have done their share of climbing apple trees." He looked over at Carl and Tim, who perked up at having been addressed.

"Why, sure," Carl said. "In fact, I'm a good climber."

"You proved that on the cliff when Nick had to come rescue you," Lucy murmured.

Carl shot her a look. "I could have gotten myself down," he said defensively. "But it was good practice for you, wasn't it, Captain Landers?"

Nick winked at Lucy over his cup. "Sure. Good practice. It isn't every day I get to rescue a young boy trapped on a cliff. Keeps my skills sharp."

"Well, you won't have to worry about that anymore as the boys still aren't allowed to leave the property," Mr. Bland said with a warning in his voice. "You men need to do what's important without having to rescue ill-mannered boys." He drank down his tea. "But you men must get some time to yourselves, don't you? Or are you here to work only and then leave when everything is finished?"

"As long as we get in the training we need, we can take off an evening," Nick said. "In fact, I've been thinking about some way to congratulate the men who have mastered some of the more difficult climbs. A reward, I guess you could say. I have about six or so that have done very well. They are even helping to train the younger GIs."

"I'd be glad to help," said Mr. Bland. "I was thinking you soldiers might want an evening of fun. I could drive you over in the truck to see a picture show in Petersburg, maybe. Then you can get yourselves an ice-cream soda while you're in town."

"Sounds good to me," Fred said. "What about you, Captain?"

"How soon can we go, sir?"

"Well, I can do it tomorrow night. I won't be working at the mill late."

"Tomorrow night," Nick said. Only then did he catch Lucy's eye. Again he sensed trouble brewing in that stare of hers. He saw her come to her feet and leave the room. He vowed then to find out if he was the cause of her discontent and prayed that God would show him what to say and do to make things right.

While Fred was engaged in a healthy conversation with Mr. Bland, Nick moseyed on outside and found Lucy lingering by the barn. He watched her for a few moments. She had on a cute dress this evening that accentuated her womanly figure. He liked the way her bobbed hair swayed around her shoulders with the evening breeze. Her hand swept the stiff boards of the barn wall as she walked about, staring up at the starlit sky.

He shoved his hands into the pockets of his trousers and ventured forward. "Nice evening."

She whirled as if his greeting had startled her. "Yes, yes it is."

"Lucy, I've been meaning to talk to you. I know it seems like all I do is eat, sleep, and run off to the camp."

"You have your work to do. I understand."

"I know, but I have a feeling that you think I'm ignoring you. That I don't appreciate everything you've done for me since I came here. But I do appreciate it, more than words can say."

She kept her gaze averted as if embarrassed by the fact. Nick sighed, wondering what else he could say to change the mood of the evening. "Also, I was thinking. I'm not a big picture show person. How about you and I get an ice-cream soda at the fountain while the others are watching the movie? I'd much rather take the time to talk to a real person over ice cream than see others talking on a screen."

Her head lifted and her gaze finally settled on him. He couldn't see her reaction well in the fading twilight, but he thought she looked pleased. "That's very nice of you to ask me, Nick, but you don't have to."

"I don't have to, but I want to. That is, unless you have other plans with your friend."

"No. I mean, he's not here. His grandfather is very ill, so he's been away to Charleston." She paused as if lost in thought. "I think it would be nice to get away for a change. I feel like I've been cooped up here. Not because of you or anything, but I haven't done anything fun in a long time and—"

"Good. I'm looking forward to it."

"I am, too."

Silence followed, but in that silence he heard things speaking loud and clear to his heart. For once he could cast aside mountaineering and army life and things military to concentrate on people. Like Lucy, who looked as if she could use a friend. And he needed a friend, as well. Someone like-minded, someone with whom he could share those hopes and dreams that God whispered in the middle of the night. Someone who would understand his beliefs and not ridicule them. And Lucy, he knew, would never ridicule anything. In fact, she would stand by closer than any friend. Or maybe she was becoming more than just a friend. If only she didn't have her other friend standing in the way.

❧

After the soldiers were dropped off at the picture show, Nick and Lucy hurried away before anyone could say anything, heading for the soda fountain around the corner. Lucy appeared relaxed and happy, chattering about the community, the shops, and the places where she used to come as a little girl. Nick preferred hearing her sweet feminine voice over the gruff voices of soldiers complaining about this or that. Once inside the shop, they settled on revolving stools at the counter with their sodas. Her chatter came to an abrupt end as she played with her straw. Nick wondered about it. At least he didn't have to worry about this being a Dear John encounter like he'd had with Donna. Instead, he hoped this might be the beginning of something special in his life. Away from the mountains and his work, he could take time to concentrate on things that he had sacrificed to duty, like the woman sitting beside him.

"So your family lives in Colorado?" Lucy finally asked, still playing with the straw in her soda. "You probably don't see them much."

"Not very often. We've never been close, not since I took up with mountaineering and then joined the army. Dad wanted me to work in his clothing business. But I had no interest in it. Can you see me in a shop, working as a tailor?"

Lucy giggled. "Not at all. You look like you belong in the mountains. You have such confidence in everything you do. Though you must get scared sometimes, don't you? I mean, it's not all fun, is it?"

"Everyone has their fears and their times of trouble. That's why I try to tell the men about God, even though it irritates Fred. He doesn't believe, you see. He thinks religion is a lot of hogwash. But I think one day he might change his mind, especially when we head over and see what's happening with the war."

"You think you will be sent to Europe soon?"

"From what I've been hearing, it's a good possibility. Rumors are running wild about a major invasion to take place in the future. It has to come sometime. Someday we'll have to drive the enemy out of those countries. When that happens, they're going to need every man."

Lucy dipped her straw down in the tall glass. "I'll miss you, Nick. I mean, I'll miss you when you leave to go back to Colorado or wherever you go. You probably will soon, won't you? The training is only supposed to last for a few weeks, if I remember."

"We may have another week or two. Depends on how quickly the men progress. There may be more units coming in with fresh instructors. But yes, my time here will eventually come to an end." For some reason the fact saddened him. He was enjoying his stay—the simplistic lifestyle, the beauty of Seneca Rocks and the surrounding mountains, even if the mountains weren't the rugged Rockies he knew so well. He liked mountains he could easily conquer without having to push himself to the limit. And he enjoyed the people, like Lucy and her family, who blessed him with their hospitality. God had provided for him every step of the way. How he wished he could do something in return for the Bland family, who had given him so much. But what? They had refused money. Maybe this time spent with Lucy would give him a chance to convey some measure of gratefulness for all she and her family had done.

"Let's take a walk around the town," Lucy suggested when they finished their sodas.

Nick jumped at the suggestion, took up her sweater, and helped her put it on. Lucy seemed surprised and pleased by the gesture, offering a shy "Thank you" in response. They slipped outside where people roamed the sidewalks, including a few military personnel.

"It looks like the U.S. Army has definitely set up residence here," Lucy observed. "We never saw anything like this a month ago. Hard to believe that our little corner of West Virginia could attract this much attention."

"This is a great area of the country for training, Lucy, not only at Seneca Rocks but in other remote places, as well. But it won't be for long. Soon we'll all be gone and it will just be a memory." Again he didn't know why the fact of his departure saddened him. Lucy must be affecting him more than he realized. He had tried to push away any thought of a relationship because of his work and her friend who seemed set in his ways. But Lucy had said many times that she and the man were only friends from long ago. There were no romantic entanglements to be had. And in all honesty, his work was well in hand. He should offer his feelings before God to see if something else was at work in his heart.

Lucy talked of the time she had come to town when her brothers were lost. The family spent a whole afternoon looking for them. "We found them in the candy store with the sheriff," she said. "Carl had been caught trying to steal candy."

"Those two have a knack for getting into trouble," Nick observed.

They continued walking until the road eventually led out of the business section of town and into a quiet area. A few homes stood near the banks of the North Fork River. Just then Nick heard a rooster crow. He laughed. "I think that bird is a little late. Either that or very early."

Lucy chuckled. "I don't know, Nick, but every time you laugh, I just have to laugh, too. It's such a hearty laugh. I hope you never lose it, no matter where you go. Laughter is as good as medicine, or so the Bible says."

Nick paused in his steps. Lucy continued on, unaware he had stopped until she turned around. "Nick? Why are you back there?"

"Lucy, I wish we had more time to spend together. I wish I didn't have to go back to camp every day. I think you're a fascinating, wonderful woman who's been overlooked by her family because of a busy lifestyle and two brothers who don't know anything but mischief."

"It's not that bad," she began.

Nick came forward. The urge to comfort her was too great. She needed to know that someone cared for her as a person. That most of all, *he* cared. His arms surrounded her. She did not stir or even quake but seemed to melt in his arms as if she had been anticipating the encounter. When they kissed, he felt more alive than ever before. This was much better than conquering a steep mountain slope. He felt renewed. If only he didn't sense despair at the same time. How could he fall in love with Lucy when he might never see her again? How could this be right?

Lucy said nothing as they turned and began heading back toward the business section of town. When her hand slipped into his, he knew she didn't mind what was happening between them and even welcomed it. He welcomed it, too— for the time being—and prayed that God would give him peace, despite an uncertain future.

eleven

Lucy felt as if she were floating on a cloud. All the doubts, the wondering, the questions about how Nick felt were answered in one starlit evening in Petersburg. She thought about it all that night and all the next day. Earlier that morning she'd gotten up to make Nick a special breakfast. He offered his usual bright smile at the fluffy pancakes and sausage waiting for him. He whispered what a special night it was for him. She told him it was for her, too. And when she saw him off to camp, he gave her a small peck on the cheek. It was nothing like the kiss they shared the evening before in Petersburg, but it still held a measure of love that welled up with each passing moment.

A song of praise filled her lips as she went about the morning chores. Nothing about the day seemed cumbersome at all with love like sugar racing through her. Thankfully, Momma said nothing about her cheerful mood. Even her brothers managed to stay out of the way. Daddy had given them the chore of digging a new garden patch for next year. All was peaceful. Her heart overflowed with joy. The doubts had been laid to rest. Nick was her love for life.

Lucy had just pulled out the jar of flour to make some muffins when she saw Carl running across the front yard and to the house. "Oh, Lu! You got a visitor!"

In an instant she thought Nick had returned to say they'd given him the day off and to ask if she would like to go somewhere. Maybe to Smoke Hole and the cave there or up into the mountains for a day all to themselves. She wiped her hands on a towel and went to the front door. Standing behind the screen with a smile on his face was Allen, all dressed up in a suit. In his hand he held a bouquet of flowers. Immediately the sense of peace drained out of her and was quickly replaced by anxiety. Her knees grew weak. She held on to the doorway to steady herself. "Allen," she managed to choke out.

"I'm back, Lucy. Finally." He gave her the bunch of daisies.

"Thank you. How—how is your granddad?"

"He's doing better. We all thought he was going to pass away at any moment, but he has a will to live. He says he wants to see us married." Allen cracked a grin. "Guess that was reason enough to keep him in the land of the living."

Suddenly the flowers lay on the ground at her feet. Lucy hurried to gather them up. "I don't know why he would think that," she murmured, heading off the kitchen to place the bouquet in a glass of water.

Allen followed. "What do you mean? Of course I've been thinking about it for weeks now, though nothing has worked out the way I planned. But today is a new day." He smiled. "So put on your best dress, Lucy. I'm taking you for a ride in the country and then to a nice dinner. I saw your mother on my way here, and she agreed to give you the day off."

Oh, no! Dear God, what am I going to do? Help me. She glanced out the window, wishing Nick were here to take her in his arms and tell Allen the news—that they were in love. Heat filled her cheeks and they felt as if they were on fire. "I—I'm surprised she would say that. I have a lot of work to do."

Allen pulled up a chair and plunked down at the kitchen table. "You always have work to do, Lucy. That's why you need some time away. With me. I need time, too. We've been apart for too long now. And I plan to have things work out, to have that date I promised you and everything else, if you catch my meaning."

"I understand that things can happen, Allen. Things change. People change, too." *Other loves can come up. Oh, how I wish you'd fallen for another girl. One in Elkins or your granddad's next-door neighbor in Charleston. Anything.*

She heard the door bump open. Carl came trotting in, looking for something to drink. "Hey, Allen! Boy, are you all fancied up."

"Sure am. I plan to take your sister to a nice place for dinner tonight. After a drive in the country."

Carl laughed. "You'd better stand in line then."

Allen chuckled. "Oh, really? What's that supposed to mean?"

"It means that Carl had better get back outside right now or Daddy's sure to find out he hasn't done the work he's supposed to do," Lucy said, throwing Carl what she hoped was a look of warning.

"I can get something to drink if I want," he retorted. "So did you tell Allen about the soldier we got staying here, Lucy? And how you went out with him to the movie last night?"

"That's enough." Lucy pushed Carl out of the kitchen. "Just for that, I'll tell Daddy everything about your cigarettes," she hissed.

Carl said no more but left abruptly with a cunning smile plastered on his youthful face. When Lucy returned to the kitchen, she felt Allen's gaze burrowing into her. "What was that all about?"

"You know Carl. He makes mountains out of molehills. Daddy took some soldiers into town last night to see a picture show. And I went along for the ride. I wanted to do something different."

Allen said nothing for a moment or two as he studied Lucy. He began to stir in his seat. "So you have some soldier living here?"

"Just temporarily. It was all Daddy's idea. He wanted to do something for the cause. So he invited one of the officers to stay here at the house so he wouldn't have to sleep in a leaky tent. It's nothing to worry about."

"Well, I do worry when I hear that you were out with another man. So tell me it isn't true, Lucy, that you didn't go out with some soldier. We can forget what Carl said—he's just a nuisance anyway—and we can have ourselves a fine day."

Oh, God, it wasn't supposed to happen like this. But what other way is there? I have to be honest with Allen. I can't go on deceiving him. "Okay, I'll tell you the truth, Allen. This is hard for me to say. I value our friendship so much. We've been through everything together. You're my best friend in so many ways. I've known you forever, it seems. But when Nick came along. . ."

Allen flew to his feet. His face turned red. He clenched his hand.

Oh, God, help me. "A—Allen, you and I are the best of friends," she managed to continue. "I—I want to stay on being good friends. But that's all."

"You can't mean that," he began. "You knew all along I was going to propose to you. That I meant to propose to you that day by the river when those two soldiers came and ruined everything." He stopped. "It's one of them you're sweet on, isn't it?" He whirled on one foot, striding out into the foyer.

"Allen, please. I do love you, but it's not a love that one can build a marriage on. I love our friendship, the great times we've had together, and our long talks. You're a great friend."

"I don't want to be your friend, Lucy. I—I want to be your husband."

"Allen, I'm so sorry. It just isn't meant to be."

"No." He looked at her, his eyes blazing. "It's not true. It can't be true. Lucy, we've known each other since we were kids. Everyone expects us to get married. My parents, Granddad, the neighbors who come to my dad's store—even your mother. They're all talking about it." His voice began to tremble. "You'll put Granddad in his grave if he hears this. He's staying alive just to see us get married."

"Allen, you can't say that. It isn't right."

"It isn't right what you're doing, either. You walk around like you're blind. You've been hoodwinked by that soldier. Some big man who climbs a bunch of rocks. And where does that leave you? He's gonna be gone, you know. He won't be around. He may even get himself killed. And then what? You want to give up our relationship to be with someone like that? Someone who won't even be there for you?" He shook his head.

"But Nick will be there. In a different way."

Once more his fist tightened. "No. We're supposed to be together, and that's the way it's gonna be." He hurried out, the screen door slamming behind him.

Lucy collapsed into the nearest chair. Tears filled her eyes. *Oh, God, what should I do? I don't know what to do.*

❧

Despite the day's promising start—a wholesome breakfast and a heartwarming farewell from Lucy—Nick had his hands full at the rocks. Today he was starting a new group, and the men proved more challenging than any group he'd worked with. Nearly every man balked at climbing the first pitch, despite the preparations back at the camp and the words of encouragement.

"Private Stacy, you did fine on the wooden corncrib," Nick said, trying not to sound exasperated. "This is no different, except this is made of rock not wood. In fact, it's unmovable."

"It's a lot different, sir. One slip and that's the end. I never thought I would die on a rock. Maybe on a battlefield, but not like this. And it looks really steep."

Nick wanted to scold him for an attitude that only bred fear. He told them no one was going to die, that they would be roped in and with a safety rope as backup. The man still hesitated, so much so that Nick panicked over the loss of time. Just as he managed to convince the soldier to try the climb, another private broke down from the stress, the tears running down his cheeks. Nick sighed, sifting through his hair with his hand. He wished at that moment he was back at the soda fountain with Lucy, sipping a cold float and talking about their future.

"So what are we gonna do about them, Captain?" Fred asked, puffing from the work of belaying. "Personally, I think they should be written up. When they became part of the MTG, they knew what they were getting into."

Nick gazed up at the rock face before him. Maybe he could find a shorter, easier route. An area that could be done without the ropes, yet they would use the ropes for safety and security. Something to instill confidence so the men would be able to tackle a pitch of this degree.

"Yes, I could write them up, but that won't accomplish much, will it? Will it make them climb? No. I'll try an easier route first. You work with the ones who have already demonstrated good technique. I'll take the other men with me and see what I can find that they will be able to climb."

"You're going to need me to hold the safety rope when they get caught up there and you're left hauling them back down," Fred retorted over his shoulder.

Nick didn't even want think about having to do another rescue if one of the men froze. There had to be an easy route for them to gain their confidence. He acknowledged the two privates still discussing their fears and anxieties with each other and ordered them to pick up their gear and follow him. Nick retraced the steps back down the path and along a narrow stretch of trail that circled the base of the rocks.

"What are we gonna do, Captain?" asked one of privates.

"We're going to climb these rocks. That's what we're here to do. But I also know it takes practice. Sometimes it's better to start with something easier. We're going to find a pitch that can be done just like the tower back at camp. Then you can say you did it, right?"

The men looked at each other and nodded. "Yes, sir."

Nick sighed, praying that God would show him the right rock. He halted then before a cliff face. Pitons had already been driven in from an earlier climb. The pitch was only about thirty feet up. Easy to negotiate and easy to get out of if necessary. He began unwinding the rope. "Looks like we have a good one here to start with, men."

"I think someone's coming, sir," one of the privates said.

Nick glanced over his shoulder to find a man quickly approaching on the trail, puffing hard from the ascent. He was dressed in a suit. *Another newspaper reporter,* Nick noted in dismay. He'd heard of reporters from the big cities, making their way to the rural area, looking to cover the training going on in the East. "Can I help you?"

"I'm looking for someone named Nick. The one staying at the Blands' house?"

"That's me. If you're here for an interview, I can talk with you later when we return to camp. I'm assisting these men with the climb right now."

Before he realized what was happening, the man rushed forward. Nick felt a sharp pain in his face. The punch drove him to the ground. The next thing he knew he was looking up at the sky, which then became hidden by the man's snarling face. Dazed by the blow, Nick felt his shirtfront pulled taut and the man's fist pummeling him until the privates managed to drag the man away. Nick slowly sat up, his head throbbing, pain radiating from his jaw. He tasted blood and felt fragments of tooth in his mouth.

The man fought his way out of the privates' grasp. "That's a warning, soldier boy," he growled. "Lucy is my fiancée, and I won't have you anywhere near her. Stay away from my girl or next time you'll get my shotgun." The man whirled and took off down the trail.

Nick sat on the ground, rubbing his bruised jaw as the privates stared down at him in bewilderment. "Are you all right, sir? Should we go back down to the camp and get the MP? Or fetch the medic?"

"No." Slowly, Nick stood to his feet. His legs began to buckle. Everything was spinning. "Sorry, men, but I—I can't take you on the rocks. Go back to Sergeant Watkins over on the other side."

"Sir, are you sure we shouldn't get some help?"

"No. I need to head back down to camp." Nick managed

to grab his backpack and the rope before stumbling down the trail. Everything was a blur. He could barely see the trail in front of him. His jaw was on fire. His tongue ran over the jagged edges of the broken tooth. He felt stunned and confused. Never had anything like this happened to him before. And right in front of the other GIs. . . He paused, squeezing his eyes shut. The humiliation of the event was worse than the pain in his battered jaw. He stumbled on, nearly tripping over the roots and brambles in his way. Even with all the mountain climbing he had done and the excruciating physical demands on his body, he'd never felt worse than he did at this moment.

Once Nick arrived at the camp and was examined, the medic told him he had suffered a concussion when he fell. The medic pulled what was left of Nick's broken tooth, then found an ice pack for his face. Nick was ordered to rest in the hospital tent for the remainder of the day. Several times the medic came and flashed a light in his eyes while asking him dumb questions. The ice felt good, but his heart felt broken. How could he have allowed things to come to this?

Later that evening, Fred popped in to check on him. "How are you doing, Captain?"

"I have a bruised jaw, a missing tooth, and a whopping headache."

Fred shook his head. "I heard what happened. What did you do to land yourself in a pickle jar like that, Captain? Why did that man come after you?"

Nick refused to tell Fred what happened last night in Petersburg. He would only rub it in his face and tell him he deserved it. Instead he stayed silent.

"Were you and that dame cozying up or something? I

mean. . .it was the same fellow we met in that field when we first got here, right?"

"Just leave it alone, Fred."

"I'm sorry, Captain, but the whole camp is buzzing over what happened—how you got yourself hooked up with a local girl, the one whose house you're staying at. Some are even accusing you of shacking up with her."

At this, Nick struggled to sit up on the cot. The ice pack fell into his lap. "None of that is true! Whoever is spreading that kind of bald-faced lie, I'll write them up. Who are they, Fred?"

"Everyone is going a bit crazy with this thing. And those two raw privates who saw it all are telling everyone about it. Captain, speaking as your friend, this is one big mess you've gotten yourself into. I heard they're going to have another trainer transferred from Elkins to take your place for a few days while you recover. Your rock climbing escapades are over for now."

Nick lay back down and closed his eyes. "Thanks for all the good news. Right now I need to rest and think things through."

"Okay, sure. Take it easy."

Nick did not reply. There was nothing to say. Nothing but regret. How could he have let this happen? Why didn't he press Lucy for more information about her relationship with this man, a supposed friend who was really her fiancé? He'd had an inkling that a relationship with her might be unwise. Now he had the bruises to prove it.

Nick sighed. He didn't know where to begin or end or even what to do. Only life had been stopped dead in its tracks by a fist and threats from an angry soul. Confusion and turmoil reigned in his heart.

twelve

I'm sorry, God. I let You down. I should have never opened myself up like I did without knowing everything. I should have never kissed Lucy. It was wrong. If I had known she was engaged, I never would have done it. He said it repeatedly to himself, but none of the words brought comfort. All he felt was pain. Looking in the mirror, the agony within matched the huge bruise extending across his jaw, which was rapidly turning black and purple. It was a stain on his being, a mark that everyone could see. He'd never felt so ashamed. He was always the proud Nick Landers, conquering hero to the masses. But he couldn't conquer this mountain. It proved too steep, too difficult, even for him. Maybe it wasn't meant to be conquered. Maybe he had deluded himself into thinking that Lucy could be his, that she was free and could even one day be his wife. All his dreams had been shattered by a fist and the humiliation it brought.

Nick found it difficult coming out of the tent the next morning. When he did, he was met with stares. Some who had not heard what happened asked if the bruise came from a tumble on the rocks. When he told them no, his voice harsher than he intended, the privates scurried away like frightened mice into the corners of the camp.

Nick sat at the table, alone in the mess tent, nursing a cup of coffee and trying to cope with the stress that seemed to follow him everywhere. He only looked up when Fred took a seat opposite him. "I'm in no mood for a lecture," he muttered.

"I don't intend to say anything, Captain. I'm only here to inquire about the day's training since your substitute hasn't arrived yet. And to ask how you're doing."

Nick hadn't given the training a thought. The men needed to continue their routine, of course. There was still his duty as an officer and to the men he vowed he would train. Without proper instruction their lives could be placed in peril. He swallowed down some coffee. "Just do the same thing as yesterday. And try to get those other boys to do the climb."

"They actually did make the climb, you know. After you left, Private Stacy and the other fellow even did the more difficult one. I was rather surprised, I must say. So do you think you're well enough to lead?"

Nick shrugged. His heart and mind certainly weren't, even if the dizziness had subsided. The medic cleared him to observe but not to rock climb. "The medic said I need to take a few days to recover, what with the concussion and all. You'll have to wait for another trainer to help out."

"They're sending someone from the climbing school in Elkins." Fred slowly ate the cereal that resembled mush in his bowl. "It won't be the same, though." He set down his spoon. "I know we've had our differences in the past, sir. But I will admit that I admire you and your skill. Okay, so I ragged on your religion. But all in all, you're an excellent officer. I won't have anyone tell you otherwise, either, or I'll punch him in the nose."

Nick stared into the eyes of his friend. A genuineness radiated from them. He had never heard Fred speak this way. He figured the man would only ridicule him for getting involved in a local spat over a girl. This new side of Fred was a surprise, to say the least—almost as much as being slugged by Lucy's irate fiancé. "I appreciate that, Fred."

Fred picked up his bowl and stood to his feet. "I just wanted you to know."

"Thanks," he said again. "It means a lot to me." The comments did cheer him, even if he remained plagued by his circumstances.

Now he considered the day's duties. He wondered what the members of the Bland family would think with him not returning to their home last night. He would have to go back to the house and retrieve his belongings. Looking at his watch, he saw he had plenty of time. The men would be engaged in their morning routine. Drill and a climb up the wooden beehive, as Lucy called it.

Nick closed his eyes. *Lucy, why didn't you tell me you were engaged?* His anger rose. *Why did you open yourself up like that? Why tell me the man was just a friend when he was your fiancé?* He couldn't help the anger of betrayal and especially from one who professed to being a Christian. How could she deceive him like this?

Nick rose weightily to his feet. He would go right now to the Blands' house to fetch his duffel bag and anything else he'd left there. And when he left Seneca Rocks of West Virginia, he would never look back.

❧

On the way to the Blands' house, Nick thought about what he might say or do should he encounter any of the family. Everyone must know by now what had happened. He prayed the family would be busy so he could sneak inside the place and grab his belongings without a confrontation. When he arrived he hid behind a tree, observing the house. Not long ago he saw Mrs. Bland and the two boys leave. He hadn't seen Lucy. He might be able to deal with her if the need arose. But what he really wanted to do was disappear and pretend none of this had ever happened.

After waiting for a bit, Nick decided to enter the house through a side door. He had a key but found the door unlocked. Walking softly upstairs, he found his belongings where he had left them and quickly stuffed them into the duffel bag. He thought of leaving a note of thanks but decided against it. He would write to the family once he returned to camp. If he could avoid seeing anyone, all the better. Glancing around the room, his gaze fell on the mirror and the ugly bruise on his jaw. He shuddered and turned away, heading down the stairs.

"Captain Landers?"

Nick froze on the landing. The deep voice came from the kitchen area. He glanced around the corner to see Mr. Bland sitting at the table, looking at a newspaper.

"Come in and have a cup of coffee with me."

"I, uh. . ." He paused. "I really need to get back to camp, sir. I have things to do and—"

"You have a few moments to spare, I'm sure." Mr. Bland folded the newspaper and gestured toward the chair opposite him.

Nick didn't know what to do. He could leave, but his spirit told him to remain, to confront the man and whatever lay before him. He sought for the words to speak as he slowly walked over and sunk down into a chair.

"That's a nasty bruise you've got there," Mr. Bland observed, pouring him a cup of coffee. He pushed the sugar and milk toward Nick. "I guess I shouldn't ask how you got it."

"That would be better, sir," Nick said dolefully, dumping

cream and sugar into the cup.

"And how are the troops progressing on the rocks?"

"Pretty well, sir. Of course there are a few who would rather be doing something else." *Like me*, he added silently, wishing he were anywhere but here conversing with Lucy's father.

"I think that's always the case when someone tries something new. I've had a few men who didn't want to work the saw at the mill. Afraid it would cut off their hand or something, I suppose. Once I showed them how to work it, taking it all step by step, they learned. And now they run it better than me." He chuckled. "Of course I didn't plan to be replaced by the younger ones. But they can quickly develop a talent for things. Just as I know you have a talent for what you do."

Nick wasn't sure where this conversation was heading.

"You know, things aren't always as they appear to be. I'm sure you've come to realize that, not only in the army but in life in general. Like with climbing rocks. They look tough, but there are ways to master them."

"Yes, sir. One needs to learn the technique."

"I guess one can say that for relationships, as well. Take, for instance, my daughter, Lucy."

He felt a shiver race through him and then heat build up. He set down the coffee cup, fighting to control the tremors in his hands.

"There are ways to handle relationships," he went on. "Ways to be a gentleman in all things."

"Yes, sir. I agree."

"And there are ways that can harm and even destroy the virtue of an innocent woman."

Nick sensed the rising condemnation. "Sir, let me say right now that I did nothing improper concerning your daughter.

We only went for a walk that evening in Petersburg. While I confess we shared one kiss, I would have never done it had I known she was engaged."

Mr. Bland sat back. "Engaged? Lucy? To whom, may I ask?"

"Why, that fellow there. That friend of hers. I think his name is Allen."

Mr. Bland shook his head. "Lucy isn't engaged. I don't know where you came up with that idea."

"He told me they were. After he landed one on me, saying if I didn't stop seeing her, I'd be greeted with a shotgun next. Mr. Bland, I'm not here to cause trouble. I deeply regret it if I have." He stood to his feet. "You have no reason to be afraid for your daughter's virtue, at least not from me. I will take my things and go back to camp where I belong. I appreciate very much your hospitality, but I don't want to cause any more pain in your family."

Mr. Bland began to unfold the newspaper once more. "All right. But I'm wondering when you plan on telling Lucy you're leaving."

Nick stood still, blinking in astonishment, wondering if he'd heard him right. "Excuse me, sir?"

"I think you owe her that, don't you? Especially since she's been caught between two men—one she thinks of as a friend, like Allen, and one she thinks she might want to marry one day. And I'm sure after giving her that kiss, you were thinking along the same line, weren't you? I mean, I don't take kissing lightly. I think of it as the start of a commitment, you see. Many young people here, they kiss and carry on without even thinking about a commitment. But I'm a believer of commitment. I believe when you decide on that kind of contact, that you mean it to last."

"I. . ." Nick didn't know what to say for fear he might offend the man even more. "I'm not sure, sir. I know for a fact that Lucy cared about my mission here. She did her best to make me feel welcome. At first I thought it was some kind of infatuation. But I believed God was doing something greater. That is, until Allen came after me yesterday."

"Allen and Lucy have known each other a long time. He likely felt he was defending her, wrong or not. And I'm sure you know, as a Christian man, that you need to forgive him for what he did to you."

"Yes, I realize that."

"If you can find the strength to forgive him, you can forgive Lucy, as well, for any hurt you think she may have caused. And before you leave for wherever the Lord sends you, you will at least say something to her about all this and where it has led the two of you." He then turned to scan the paper once more.

Nick pondered Mr. Bland's advice for a moment before setting the house key on the table, issuing a quiet "thank you," and moving off to the back door. He couldn't quite believe the conversation. Here he had thought Lucy's father would supplement the blow Allen had delivered, with a rain of harsh words—that Mr. Bland considered him a vulture, implanting talons in his daughter's heart. But it seemed Mr. Bland liked the idea of their being together, that things were not as they appeared. And Lucy felt the same way.

Nick returned to camp, wondering where to go from here. Forget training the men for the moment. He still had a tough climb ahead of him, one of the soul and spirit. He had to decide what tactics he would need to master this steep pitch of emotion. Vanish into thin air as he had proposed to do before he met with Mr. Bland? Or seek out Lucy after the day's events were complete to try to figure out the future? Should he use tactics of kindness and gentle persuasion? Or come right out and ask her intentions?

Nick decided to check on how the training was progressing at Seneca Rocks. In the distance he spotted the men positioned along the rocks like a line of ants, becoming ever clearer as he approached. When he arrived, Fred was on the safety rope as usual. He said nothing, even when Fred gave him a questioning glance, until the last climber had safely reached the first pitch and the command "off belay" was given.

Fred loosened the rope twisted around his waist. "Where were you off to? I noticed you had disappeared."

"I went to get my duffel bag from the Blands' house."

Fred raised an eyebrow. "That must have been an adventure. You didn't run into that fellow again, did you?"

"No. Only Lucy's father."

Fred whistled while reaching for his canteen to take a swallow of water. "That must have been an interesting encounter."

"Actually, it was. It appears he's not entirely against Lucy and I being together."

"What?"

"At least that's what I gathered from the conversation. And Lucy is not engaged, even though Allen said they were."

"I guess that lets you breathe a little easier, eh, Captain?"

"Not much," Nick admitted. "I still need to figure out what to do. He wants me to talk to Lucy. But I know we'll soon be leaving, Fred. I can't continue a relationship from across the country or even the ocean. If we get sent to the front, which seems likely, then there really isn't a reason to pursue this."

"Then, my friend, you should have never started anything

to begin with." Fred twisted the cap back on the canteen. He handed the rope off to Nick. "I know you can't climb, but are you up to holding the safety rope and belaying this short pitch for me? The other trainer is on the opposite side of the rocks."

Nick did so, trying to keep his attention focused as his friend began the climb to where the other men waited. He looked on as Fred felt for each hand- and foothold, using the piton to connect his carabiner, careful to do all that was required to maintain the utmost safety. He began to pray, too, that God would likewise lead him as he tried to navigate the precarious foot- and handholds in his relationship with Lucy, until he reached solid ground.

thirteen

Lucy could not imagine the changes in fortune, sending her from one extreme of emotion to the other. After the evening in Petersburg with Nick, when she'd felt the strength of his arms around her and his lips on hers, she was flying on a cloud. And now suddenly she felt herself tumbling out of control after the encounter with Allen. Whispers abounded soon after. She had not seen Allen since the meeting when he first learned of her preference for Nick over him. Nor had she seen Nick for that matter. She felt certain the two men had met somehow. When she glanced in Nick's room the next morning, she saw he had not slept in his bed, though his belongings were still there. Then when she arrived back after visiting a friend, she found all his personal items gone. A knot formed in her stomach. Somehow Allen had driven Nick away, just like he said he would. She simply had to find out what happened.

Lucy put on her best dress and even a touch of color to her lips. She wanted to look her best when she went to confront Allen. She needed confidence. Picking up her purse, she rushed out the back door, hoping no one in her family would see her. She didn't want to have to explain her every move to them. She was on God's path now, and a path she felt certain Nick and she were to walk, even if everyone else thought otherwise.

When she arrived at the store, she met a few of her neighbors, including Mrs. Sampson who gave her a bright smile.

"Well, I hear it's soon to be official, Lucy!"

She blinked. "What's that, Mrs. Sampson?"

"About you and Allen. Of course I knew it all along. You two just seemed to be a pair. I guess because I saw you two together when you were still in diapers." She chuckled.

A sick feeling came over Lucy. What was Allen telling everyone? A wave of anger gripped her as she pushed open the door. Allen stood behind the counter, his back to her, putting items on the shelf. "Allen."

He spun, the boxes he had put up on the shelf tumbling down in a shower. "Lucy, you can't come sneaking up on me like that." He began picking up boxes from the floor.

"Well, you can't be telling lies."

He looked at her over the counter and quickly stood to his feet. "Excuse me?"

Lucy put her purse on the counter. "You heard me. You're telling everyone that we're getting married."

"I didn't tell everyone. No one but the goody-goody soldier, that is. He needed to know where things stood."

Lucy stared wide eyed. "Why did you tell Nick that?"

"Because it's the truth." He looked over at a few customers who stood in the aisles, gawking at them. "Can you keep your voice down, Lucy? You're scaring the customers."

"You'd better find your father or someone to take over, because you have some explaining to do." Lucy took her purse off the counter and marched outside, plunking herself down on a bench. She nodded at the customers that entered the store. Now her gaze fell on Seneca Rocks. Dark clouds began to drift over them. She couldn't help the tears that flooded her eyes. How could Allen have done something like this—tell Nick that they were engaged? Now it made sense why Nick had left their home in such a hurry. And how he must dislike her, too, for thinking she had kept this secret from him, only to have them kiss on a street in Petersburg. She couldn't help the anger foaming up within. *Oh, God, why did this have to happen?* When she thought about it, though, she realized most of this was her fault. If she had been open and honest with Allen about her feelings from the beginning, all of this might have been avoided.

The door to the store bumped open, and Allen stumbled out. "I really need to watch the store, Lucy. Dad said he could take over for ten minutes, but that's it."

She patted the seat next to her. "Allen, come here. I need to say something."

He raised an eyebrow but he followed her lead and sat down cautiously beside her.

"I want to say I'm sorry I wasn't honest about Nick right out. All that talk about getting together and everything. I wasn't being truthful. I should have told you that I loved Nick. Like I said, you're my best friend in so many ways. But he's different. He isn't a friend. He's more like—"

"He's nothing," Allen muttered.

"No. He's everything I need in a husband. You're everything I need in a friend. You both fill different roles, and roles that are both dear to me."

Allen stood to his feet. "You think he's better than me, don't you? Just because he can climb an old rock. Well let me tell you, he sure can't defend himself. He's a fish. Weak. Can't even stand up for himself like a man. I don't know what you see in him."

Lucy stared.

"I told him to stay away from you. That we. . ." Allen

paused. "You know we're supposed to be engaged, Lucy. I just jumped the gun a bit and told him that. But he needed to know that I wanted him out of your house and your life."

Lucy flew to her feet, clutching her purse to herself. "You can't do things like that, Allen. You can't speak for me or for what God has planned for my life. And I can say that friends don't do this to one another. They don't twist arms and hearts. They understand and care for each other. They are there for each other, no matter what. I've come to realize this even more after my own error. But if you can't see it, too, then this really needs to be good-bye."

Lucy headed down the stairs of the store and out to the road. She had no idea where she was going. At this point, she didn't care. Her mind lay in a fog. She had lost everything. Allen's friendship. Nick's love. She had nothing left. She tried not to look at the rocks that only added to the misery in her heart. She didn't even look at the rows of tents in the distance that began to materialize. Even when raindrops began falling in earnest from the darkened skies, she walked on. She would continue until there was no more pain. She didn't care where she ended up, either. Even if it was in the next county.

Suddenly a horn sounded. She wiped the strings of her damp hair out of her eyes and continued walking, ignoring the vehicle that crept up beside her.

"Lucy?" a voice called out from the passenger window.

She looked up even though the rain fell harder, making it difficult to see. She couldn't believe her eyes. The voice belonged to Nick.

"What are you doing out here? Where are you going?"

"Nowhere," she said, looking away.

Nick said something to the driver, who obliged and pulled the military jeep over to the side of the road a hundred feet ahead of her. Nick jumped out. Lucy looked at him and saw a nasty bruise on his face. Her breath caught at the sight.

"You shouldn't be walking out here in the rain. And you're already starting to shiver. Come on and get into the jeep."

She shook her head. "N—no. Just go ahead, Nick. Leave me alone. That's what you did. Left me alone."

Instead of answering her, he took her by the hand and led her over to the jeep, then opened the back door. "Please get in. Stan, go ahead and drive back to the barracks. Then I will take this young lady home."

The driver obliged, taking them to the tent city where he exited the jeep. Nick took the wheel and pointed to the passenger seat beside him. Lucy slowly moved from the back to the front seat, refusing to look Nick in the eye, even if his bruised face did spawn questions. He put the vehicle into gear and sped down the road. "Where are we going?" Lucy asked. "I don't intend to go home right now."

"I'm taking you to a place where I can get you a cup of coffee. You need something warm in you before you catch cold."

"I'm not cold."

He gave her a sideways glance. "So why were you walking out there?"

"I'll give you three reasons."

"I take it I'm one of the reasons."

She paused at his honesty. "Well, yes. You left without saying a word. You just packed up your things and left. You blame me for what Allen said and it isn't right."

"Lucy, I don't blame you."

"Yes, you do. And I had nothing to do with it. I can't help it if Allen got angry and went and told you we were engaged when he knew it wasn't the truth."

"I know. Your dad told me."

At this, Lucy stared in disbelief. "You talked to Daddy?"

"It was a very good conversation. He's quite a wise man. And...I think he likes me."

Lucy couldn't help cracking a smile. "He's enjoyed having you at the house. He reads the paper all the time about the war. I think it's been good for him to talk to a soldier who's training for it. If he were younger, I'm sure he would have signed up. He holds nothing but the highest regard for you."

"I could sense it. It was like the best tonic I could get. It's hard to get any respect these days. You try to gain the respect of your soldiers. But I have to admit, since the whole incident, I've lost the respect of my men. Everyone looks at me strangely. Even with the men I used to command, there's a difference in the way they respond to me."

Lucy shook her head in confusion. "I don't understand why you're having such trouble."

"I guess you didn't hear. Your friend Allen hunted me down at the cliffs and gave me a present, right in front of my men." Nick pointed to the bruise that decorated his face.

Lucy gasped. "Oh, no! Allen did that?"

"And he told me he would come after me with a shotgun if I ever got near you again. Not that I was about to leave you on the side of the road in the rain today, even if he does come after me. I'm willing to take the risk."

"Oh, Nick, I'm so sorry. I don't know what to say."

"You don't have anything to be sorry for."

Tears welled up in her eyes. "Yes, I do. If I had been open and honest with Allen about my feelings, none of this would have happened. I led Allen on. I didn't have the courage to tell him I had fallen in love with you." There. She'd said it at last. She didn't care what Nick thought of it, either. It was all out in the open, before both men, to digest at will. No more secrets lay between any of them now.

Nick said nothing for a few moments. Finally he responded in a quiet voice. "Lucy, I'm speechless."

"You don't have to say anything. I just had to say it myself, because it's been bottled up inside me since the first day I laid eyes on you. I can't explain why, but you're someone very special to me, Nick. I know you don't feel the same way, but that's okay. I want you to know that I care about you. With everything in my heart." She hesitated. "But I think you care a little bit, too, or else you wouldn't have kissed me the other night."

Nick chuckled as he steered the jeep into a parking place at the corner diner. "Lucy, you're worth kissing. You're a wonderful, caring woman. I'll have to admit, on that street, all I wanted to do was reassure you, to let you know that I see everything you do here, even if you feel buried by the roles you play at home. Honestly, I hadn't intended to kiss you. But it seemed the right thing to do, and I still believe it was."

Before Lucy could say anything else, Nick leaned over, his face close, his lips once again seeking hers.

"Nick?" she managed to say when he withdrew, her lips still tingling from the kiss.

"I guess it was the right thing to do again, Lucy," he said with a laugh. His fingers reached out to touch her face. "You have such a sweet spirit. I only wish. . ."

"What?"

"Never mind." He pocketed the jeep key. "Let's get you that cup of coffee."

Moments later Lucy sat at the booth, nursing a cup of

coffee with the steam warming her cheeks. Not that she needed any more warmth after the tender moment with Nick in the jeep. He had also ordered a coffee and laced it with cream and sugar, four teaspoons' worth. When Lucy commented on the amount, he only shrugged. "I like my drinks sweet," he explained. "Just like my girls."

"So you've had other girls?"

"Just one. I think I told you about her. She never liked the mountains. She wasn't the rugged type. I couldn't see her putting on overalls and crossing rivers with a basket of muffins over one arm." He grinned before taking a drink of coffee.

"So where do we go from here, Nick?"

He sat back in his seat, his gaze never leaving her. "Once my mission here is accomplished, I move on, Lucy. Probably back to Colorado."

Lucy leaned forward. "Then take me with you. I think I would love Colorado, from what you've described."

Nick shook his head, fingering the cup handle. "I can't do that, Lucy. I don't know how long I will even be at Camp Hale when the call comes up. I could end up leaving for Europe. You won't know anyone in Colorado. You're better off here, with your family and the people you know. And, of course, the rocks."

Lucy sighed. "So I wait here not knowing." She then righted herself. "Then at least marry me before you leave."

Nick's mouth fell open. His hand jerked so he nearly upset his coffee cup. "Marry you?"

"Yes. Why not? At least we can have a few days of married life together. We can have a simple ceremony, maybe even at the rocks. Then I will wait for you to come back from the war."

Nick shook his head, much to her disappointment. "Lucy,

don't you think you're rushing this?"

"No. There isn't any time. I don't want to lose you, Nick. And it would settle things once and for all, as far as Allen is concerned. Please. Let's just do this before your duty and the war tear us apart."

Nick downed the rest of his coffee. "Again you leave me speechless, Miss Lucy Bland. I don't know what I can say to something like that. In fact, normally the fellow asks for the girl's hand in marriage. I don't even have a ring and—"

"I don't care. Rings don't matter to me. I don't even own any jewelry. Please, let's just do this."

Nick wiped his hand across his face and sighed. "Lucy, I wish I could come right out and say yes. But I don't know the future. You don't know the future. You could be making the worst mistake of your life."

"I trust God, Nick. And I know you do, too."

"I trust Him also with times and seasons. And when the time is right for a commitment. I—I don't believe it's that time, Lucy. We've only known each other a few weeks. You can't say you know enough about me."

"That's not true. I know you well enough to want to marry you."

"Lucy, you can't say that. Neither of us can. Only time can help."

"But it can't, Nick, don't you see? There is no time. Soon you'll be gone."

Nick came to his feet. "Speaking of which, it's getting late. I need to be heading back. I hope you understand what I need to do—that other things take priority right now."

"Of course. Duty calls." She grabbed her purse. "I only wish you would consider other duties, too, Nick. Duties that can be just as important as your rock climbing. Like duties to people." She paused. "Maybe I know now why that other girl left you. It's hard to compete with a rock wall, both on the inside and the out." To her surprise, Nick said nothing. The ride back to her home was made in silence. When she walked in the front door to the sound of the jeep driving away, the family pounced. Momma scolded Lucy for her damp dress. Carl and Tim asked about the jeep in the front yard. Daddy inquired what happened.

"Nothing, Daddy," Lucy said glumly. "Not a thing." She went to her room and flopped down on the bed. It couldn't end this way, not after all they had been through, even if it had been a mere few weeks. There had to be love there. But how could love remain, especially after her comments this night? She wished she had not said those angry words to Nick. That she had given him time to consider her request. She had been too impulsive once again, acting out of desperation propelled by anxiety. She wanted so much to marry Nick and not risk losing him. Now she may have lost him anyway.

Lucy rose from the bed and went to the desk drawer, taking out the first letter she had ever written to Nick. She found an envelope and addressed it as before. *Captain Nicholas Landers, Seneca Rocks Camp.* "At least this note will tell you my true heart, Nick," she murmured, giving the note a light kiss. "Even if there's nothing else left to hope for."

❧

A week later, Nick was gone. There was no note from him. No word at all. Lucy looked at Seneca Rocks with a thick lump in her throat, her heart heavy like stone. But the tears refused to come. Nick had made his decision. And she had made hers.

She would wait as long as she had to, just as her letter said.

fourteen

Summer 1945

Two years had come and gone. Lucy still couldn't believe how much time had slipped by. In all that time she'd only received a few letters from Nick, mostly having to do with his work in Colorado and expressing his thanks to her family for its hospitality. Nothing about the encounter at the diner where she'd confessed her true feelings or the kisses they'd shared or her plea that they marry. Nothing about the letter she sent, even, or what the future may hold. It seemed everything they had nurtured during his short time at Seneca Rocks disappeared as if nothing had ever happened.

Allen asked repeatedly for her to forgive him and to accept his proposal of marriage. Lucy politely refused, though she had met him for an occasional soda at the shop. Other men had come around, asking for dates. She had refused them, as well.

Instead, Lucy took long walks along the North Fork River. She ventured to the base of the rocks to view the pitons still there, hammered in by Nick's hand. Her feet traced the paths in the fields where tents and the massive beehive once stood. She paid homage to the place where Nick first greeted her with his dazzling smile. And then she came to the road in Petersburg when he had announced his love with a kiss. Had it all been real or just a dream? Maybe it was simply a dream and she should stop living in the past.

At least Daddy had caught wind of her unhappiness and tried to help. He taught her how to drive. He gave her a little bungalow that she could call her own. She fixed it up with some of Momma's old linens and a few pieces of furniture the family no longer needed. Lucy was glad for the tiny home that provided her a place of refuge to think about her life and her future, however bleak it seemed. Many days she would think back to that time nearly two years ago—had it been that long?—when the military men first came to climb the rocks. And dear Nick, who remained vivid in her thoughts, his words reverberating in her ears, his kiss on her lips, still fresh and inviting. Momma and Daddy had suggested many times that she let go of the past and embrace the idea of her future with another man. Even Daddy knew of a few men at the mill who wanted to ask her out on a date. But Lucy couldn't. Not until she had confirmation that Nick had indeed moved on with his life, whether by marriage to another woman or because of the war.

Eventually, Nick's letters had trickled down to nothing. Lucy had tried to discover what may have happened to him by traveling to Elkins with Daddy. There she'd sought out town officials who had records of the military units who came back from the war. With that Lucy was able to find the address for Camp Hale and wrote Nick letters. When they came back *Return to Sender*, she tried calling officials in Colorado. They could tell her nothing until late in the fall of 1944. It was then she learned the division would be sent to Italy. They took her name and address and said someone would be in touch if there was any news about Captain Nicholas Landers. All she could do from that moment on was cling to the news reports in Daddy's paper, listen to the radio, or watch the newsreels at the theater for any hint of Nick's possible whereabouts. Lucy lived her life by Seneca Rocks, waiting for any news whether good or bad.

Today she went about her duties as usual, which included watering the flowers she had planted not too long ago. Momma and she had gone into the woods and dug up wildflower roots to plant in a little garden near her tiny home. It was hard to believe that God had provided her this quaint dwelling just up the road from her parents. The house had belonged to a man who worked at the mill, and when he died of a heart attack last year, his relatives gave the bungalow to Daddy as a gift. In turn it became Lucy's.

"Wanna go for a walk, Lu?" a voice greeted her.

Lucy looked up and saw Tim standing near the road. He had grown up these past two years. Tall, with an ever-ready smile, his voice was slowly changing as he entered his teen years. While nearly sixteen-year-old Carl was entertaining a new girlfriend or asking Daddy about driving an automobile, Tim would stop by and ask to do something with her. He was still of the age to enjoy a sibling relationship. And she'd never found him as much of a nuisance as Carl. Tim had an innocence about him that she liked. She cherished their sibling bond, especially during these lonely months. "You know better than to call me Lu," Lucy warned him with a smile.

"Yeah, I know. Just wanted to see your reaction."

"I guess I could go for a walk. Let me finish watering the flowers." Lucy emptied the rest of the watering can on the plants, then set the can down by the steps. They took off down the road, heading toward Hopper General Store. Before her rose the familiar sight of Seneca Rocks. At least the rocks didn't bother Lucy as much as they had when Nick first left. She could barely look at the rocks then without shedding a tear. Now the sight had become commonplace again, just as it was before Nick had ever set foot here. A settling of things inside her heart, she'd decided.

"Let's go to the Hoppers' store," Tim said. "I want a soda. I'm thirsty."

Lucy obliged. She didn't mind going into the store now that Allen was engaged to a girl named Susan. Allen and Lucy still talked to each other, though things were never the same after the episode with Nick. As it was, Lucy had just received an invitation to Allen's wedding. At least things weren't too bad if Allen felt inclined to invite her. She thought she might have been excluded or he would be bitter over the way things ended. There was a bright spot to be had in all this, and he didn't look down on her for what she'd decided.

At that moment she did wonder about her decision. Waiting for some ghost of a man, whom she had no idea where he was or if he still existed. It seemed ludicrous. Maybe she needed to move on with her life. She had waited two years, after all. Two years of her life pining away for a man she was never meant to have. She sighed and vowed the next time a man asked her out on a date, she would accept.

Several automobiles were parked by the storefront when they arrived. People milled about sharing news. A car door opened, and a lanky man stood up. Lucy wouldn't have taken any notice except the man withdrew a pair of crutches from the backseat. Upon closer inspection, she saw that part of his leg was missing.

"He's back, Lu," Tim said with a grin. "Ha, ha! See! Gotcha good! And you didn't even see it coming."

"What are you talking about, silly?" Lucy continued walking until a voice stopped her short.

"Hi, Lucy."

She turned. The man with the crutches had greeted her. She blinked. "Do I know you?"

"Are you daft, Lu?" Tim chided, elbowing her. "He's your soldier, the one who stayed with us! That captain is back. I ran into him when I came to the store earlier. He told me to come fetch you. Surprise!"

Lucy could only stand there like a statue. Was this thin and ragged man with a scraggly beard and using crutches because of a missing leg, Nicholas Landers? Her Nick? It didn't seem real. Maybe this was just another dream like the ones she often had at night, wondering what he looked like years later.

He hobbled over on the crutches. "I know this must come as a shock," he began.

Lucy didn't know what to say or do. Finally she opened her purse and gave Tim some money to buy a few sodas. "Take your time."

"Sure." Tim winked.

They moved off to sit on a bench in front of the store. "I don't blame you for not speaking to me," Nick said, easing himself down on the bench and propping the crutches against the wall. "I decided to come back. I had to see you again."

Once more she tried to think of the words to say. Only questions filled her mind. Why did he leave without saying good-bye? Why did he cease responding to her letters? Why was there so little in the way of communication from him for almost two years? Why? But she asked none of them. She only sat in silence.

"I also wanted to come back and thank your parents for

everything they did for me. You all were such a big part of my life two years ago. You were like family to me. I owed you at least that." He paused. "I know what you're going to say: that family doesn't do these kinds of things to each other. They don't leave without a word about where they are going or what is happening. They stay in communication. They pray for each other." He looked down at the ground. "I did pray, Lucy. I could do nothing else but pray. My life was in God's hands."

"What—what happened?" she finally managed to choke out.

He glanced at his leg. "You mean this? It happened in Italy. We were under heavy enemy fire. A mortar blasted into a trench about fifty feet away. Should have taken me out. Instead the shrapnel tore off my leg. I saw my leg there and my foot, lying in the trench. An awful sight."

Lucy shivered and looked away.

"Sorry. I guess I shouldn't have gotten so descriptive. It was hard. I thought I would die, there was so much blood. I looked over at Fred and asked him to get me the medic and maybe my leg while he was at it. It was a sick joke, I know. It was so surreal. . . He didn't answer me. I said, 'Fred, c'mon, I need that medic now. I lost my leg.'" Nick hesitated. "Then I saw the blood coming from under his helmet. He had taken one in the head. He was gone."

"I'm so sorry, Nick. I know he was your friend."

Tears filled his eyes. "He was gone, just like that. Talking to me one moment. Telling me the mortar blasts were getting awfully close and asking if we should abandon our position. And then he was gone."

"I'm sorry, Nick," she said again.

"But you know, he accepted the Lord only a few months

before that. We were still in Colorado. He was on a ledge and a piton came loose. He was dangling there, a couple hundred feet above the ground. He said he saw his life flash before his eyes. And he saw how black and cold it was. After that we talked. He wanted assurance he would see life after death. So I talked to him about accepting the Lord and the gift of eternity."

"I'm so glad, Nick. That must give you comfort."

"It does a little. At least Fred is in a good place. I just wish I had gone there with him, that the mortar had taken out my heart and not my leg."

"Why?"

The question seemed to catch him off guard. She saw the confusion in his eyes. He suddenly turned quiet.

At that moment Tim returned with cold sodas for each. "So how is the reunion going? Bet you're glad you don't have to fight anymore, huh, Nick?"

"I suppose. The battlefield is a terrible place, I must say. Even in my dreams I can still hear the grenades and mortars going off. If I hear a loud truck, I think it's enemy tanks crossing the breach."

"Well, there's no enemy here," Tim said matter-of-factly. "And guess what? Did you know Lucy's been waiting for you all this time? Did you tell him, Lu, how you refused to go on any dates, even with men from Daddy's sawmill? That all you did was wait? Even Allen finally gave up and now he's getting married in a few months. We just got the invitation for it."

Lucy wanted to silence Tim, who never had any trouble sharing everything he knew in life. Yet the look Nick gave her stilled her heart. A look of wonder and maybe of gratitude. Though why he would be grateful, she wasn't certain. He'd abandoned her, after all. But looking down at his devastating wound, how could she be angry for what he'd done? She began to drink her soda. Try as she might to find mercy in this situation, the words were still hard to say.

"So how are you?" he finally asked her.

"All right. Daddy taught me how to drive. Someone at his mill died and left him this small house, which he lets me use. So now I have my own place."

"Good for you. I know how much you wanted to be out on your own."

"Do you want to see it? Can you walk that far?"

"I can walk as far as I need to," he said a bit gruffly, as if her challenge had sparked defiance in him. She told Tim she would see him later and headed out with Nick, pleased he was able to keep pace with her on his crutches. She marveled at his strength. After all his rock climbing, he must have developed strong arm muscles to pull himself up so many cliff faces. She thought about that fact and suddenly became somber. He would never be able to do those things again. He could never maneuver himself with crutches up the steep mountain trail to the top of Seneca Rocks. And certainly he wasn't in the army any longer. She glanced out the corner of her eye at his civilian shirt and navy blue trousers, so different from the green she was accustomed to him wearing. Everything had changed.

When they arrived, he was panting. Sweat rolled down his face. Lucy immediately went to fetch him a glass of water, which he accepted. "Nice place," he noted, easing himself down on the front step.

"I can bring out some chairs," Lucy began.

"I'm fine. Even if I look like I can't do anything anymore, I can do plenty."

Lucy bit her lip at the accusation his words implied. "I didn't mean—"

"I know. I'm sorry that came out the way it did. I'm just tired of people seeing me as a cripple in need of special care. My mother spent the last few months babying me. Fetching me everything. I tried to tell her I could do things for myself. She spent the day by my side, crying." He paused then. "Mourning her poor crippled son's loss, I guess."

"You aren't poor, Nick, not with the Lord on your side."

For an instant he grimaced. Lucy wondered about his response. Was Nick angry with God for what had happened? He didn't say it, but his reaction spoke volumes. Finally he murmured, "I guess," before downing the rest of his water.

"I plan to get a job," Lucy continued. "Now that I know how to drive, Daddy said there might be jobs near the mill. So I'm going to look around. I need money to get things for the house. Momma gave me a few things to get me started."

"You really have changed," he noted. "I mean, having your own house and everything. You seem to know where you're going in life, and that's good."

"What about you, Nick? Are you going to stay in Colorado?"

He snorted. "Living next to mountains I can never climb again is like having a perpetual pin stuck in me. It's nice to look at, but the idea I can't do the only thing I love—it hurts too much."

"I'm sure once you get a prosthesis, you will be able to do more."

He shrugged. "I suppose."

"I mean it won't be the same as having a real leg. But then you can get around better."

"You always were the optimist," he said with a smirk. "Lucy

coming to feed hungry soldiers with her muffins. Lucy offering to help guide. Lucy, who's always been there for me when I needed her most."

But you weren't there for me, Nick. You left me two years ago. You said nothing to me. Did you ever think of me during all that time? Did you ever wonder what I was doing? Did you have any feelings for me at all?

"But I'm not here to gain sympathy," Nick was quick to add. "I just wanted to come back and thank you all for everything. For making it a special time in my life that I will never forget."

"I'm sure Daddy and Momma would like to see you. You don't have to be anywhere, do you?"

"I'm staying with a friend in Elkins. I need to tell him I'm here somehow and what I'm doing. He's visiting a cousin who lives near here. Sadie Mahone."

"I know Sadie. We can call her on the telephone and let her know that you will be staying for supper, and she can give the information to your friend. Then he can come by and pick you up. If that's all right."

Nick nodded. "That would be great, Lucy. Kind of like old times. . ." He hesitated, then added, "Having a meal together and all." He took up his crutches and maneuvered himself to a standing position. Lucy couldn't help watching. She bit her lip to keep her emotions at bay. Maybe it was better that they had this final good-bye. Or was it really good-bye? Maybe it was really a "Hello, I'm back to stay." *If you will only forgive, Lucy, and open your heart up to a man who has lost so much.* She did not know what the outcome might be. Once again her future lay with God and with Nick.

❧

Nick's presence in the Blands' home seemed to humble them

all. Carl, in particular, appeared upset by what had happened to Nick. At first Carl wanted to hear all the news of the war. When he learned the details of Nick's wound and Fred's death, he turned silent. Tim was the more positive one out of them all, encouraging Nick to get a prosthesis and keep living life to the fullest. Lucy marveled at how her brothers had changed since the days when they were nothing but trouble.

Daddy and Momma both sat and listened carefully to everything Nick shared, offering a sympathetic ear and plenty of good food, which Nick appeared to enjoy. Yet a distinct sadness prevailed. Nick had changed so much. It was not only the wound to his leg that ailed him but some untold wound to his soul.

After the meal, Momma shooed Lucy out of the kitchen, claiming she would do the dishes. Daddy also left them alone and went seeking his paper. Lucy and Nick took seats outside on the porch to enjoy the nice evening.

"It was good to see everyone again," he commented. "Carl and Tim have grown up quite a bit."

"Yes. I think life itself got them thinking about where they are going and what they will do."

"War is also an eye-opener. I didn't really know what I was getting myself into. I thought all my skill in mountaineering would save me. But when the fire rains down, nothing can save you except the hand of God. I guess I should be happy that I'm alive. But right now I'm not sure what I'm living for."

"God isn't done with you yet, Nick Landers. He still has a plan for your life."

Nick sighed. "I'm not sure what a one-legged man can

do. The life I used to know is gone forever. Hard to believe. Sometimes I can't quite believe it myself. But I know I have to wake up one day and accept it."

Lucy sat still for a moment, praying for the words to say. From here she could make out the image of Seneca Rocks through the tree branches. "The rocks are still the same, no matter what happens," she commented.

"What?"

"Seneca Rocks. They stay the same. Even when it snows, rains, or the sun is shining on them, they never change. They may look different, but in essence they remain the same. You're still the same, Nick. You may have gone through storms. You may have only one leg right now. But the same Nick is there, the man God made. And the same man God can still use, if you let Him. The trials get us ready for a greater purpose. You're still the same man who trained all those young men to get over their fears. The same man who helped lead a lost person to Christ before he died. And the same man who still has so much to live for."

Silence met her ears except for the occasional scraping of a few branches against the side of the house. Lucy thought she heard a sniff. Was Nick crying? She looked over, but the shadows of the falling dusk masked his face.

Just then a car pulled up. Nick slowly came to his feet. "My ride."

"Will I see you tomorrow?" Lucy asked.

For a moment he stood there, balancing on the crutches, weighing everything. Her heart began to patter. She knew he was considering everything—the past, the present, the future. He stared off toward Seneca Rocks as if studying them. He took a step forward. Her heart began to flutter. Then just as quickly, he shook his head. "I can't, Lucy. Thanks for everything. I mean it sincerely."

Her heart sank. Tears welled up in her eyes as he hobbled away. When the car door slammed shut, she knew he had shut the door for the last time. There was no turning back or going forward. "Good-bye forever, Nick," she whispered and ran off to shed her tears.

fifteen

Lucy thought it a fine plan that sunny afternoon a few days later—to take a picnic lunch and make peace with her troubled heart by the rocks she had known all her life. Seneca Rocks. The rocks that had brought Nick to her and then suddenly sent him away. But it was not really the rocks that did it. Or her. Or even God. It was meant to be this way. She believed it. She had kept her end of the bargain. She had waited until they were reunited. Nick had come back alive, even if he was missing a part of his limb and his heart. And he had made his decision.

Lucy folded a red gingham cloth to cover the contents of the basket. It seemed hard to believe she'd decided to bring food with her on this journey, as if she could eat one bite. But it seemed the right thing to do. She'd even baked a few muffins. Packed bread and cheese. A bottle of milk. The basket was heavy, but she would bear it. She would offer it all to God and find her happiness and her worth in Him as she broke bread.

Picking up the handle to the basket, Lucy began the trek toward the famous rocks that seemed to beckon to her. She felt strength surge through her. Suddenly the basket didn't feel as heavy anymore. She felt light on her feet. God was already doing a work of restoration. Giving her the oil of joy for mourning. Giving her a thankful heart.

Just then Lucy heard a car horn sound. She prayed it wasn't

a neighbor looking to spy on her and ask her questions. Or Allen, though she had not seen him for quite a while. She turned to see who it was and caught sight of a familiar face in the passenger seat.

Nick.

Her heart nearly stopped.

The car pulled over. Nick whispered something to the driver, then opened the door.

"Wherever you plan on going, I'd sure like to come along."

Lucy stared as he took out the crutches. She didn't know what to say. Finally, she blurted out, "I—I was going on a picnic."

"Really. With whom?"

"With no one. No one, that is, except God. I mean, He isn't no one, but, oh, never mind."

His face broke into a smile. Oh, how she loved his smile. It was in her every dream from the first day she'd laid eyes on him. "I wonder if I dare ask if it's all right for me to come along."

"I'm sure He won't mind."

Nick turned to address the driver. When they came to some manner of agreement, he rose out of the car using his crutches. As they entered the field, Nick kept up with her pace for pace. When they reached the river, he found a rock to sit down on. "Need a little breather," he said.

"This is as good a spot as any," Lucy announced, spreading the red gingham cloth onto the grass and placing food upon it. When she produced the muffins, Nick stared in shock and amazement.

"You didn't know I was still around, did you?"

"No. I made them for me. Well, and for God. Sort of a peace offering. I was going to come here and. . ." She hesitated.

What was she going to do? "I was going to offer everything to God. Everything from the last few years." She hesitated. "But I thought—I thought you were leaving for good."

"I considered it. Where would I go, really? Then I said to myself, how can I leave the one woman who cared for me? Why should I abandon her again and hurt her heart and mine? I would be throwing everything away. I've already lost enough. I wasn't going to lose you, too. Then it really would have been the end of me. Because, Lucy Bland, you mean everything to me."

Lucy blushed and handed him a muffin. "Here."

"I don't suppose you would mind a trade?"

Lucy stared wide-eyed as he withdrew a simple box from his pocket. She couldn't believe she was actually seeing this. "That isn't what I think it is," she began.

"It's just an idea I have. I know we haven't spoken much since I left. That we still have a lot to learn about each other. But this is a token of a promise and one I intend to keep with all my heart, if you'll let me." He showed her the ring. "This is my promise like the one you made me. That I will be there for you always, Lucy. I won't turn away. I will do whatever I must to fulfill my destiny, with you by my side. And I believe the mountains can still be a part of it all."

"Oh, Nick," Lucy said softly, taking the ring. "It's so beautiful."

"I bought it back in Colorado," he confessed.

"What? In Colorado? But. . ." His statement confused her. He had left the first time without even saying good-bye. They had hardly remained in contact but for a few scant letters. And hadn't he said good-bye just the other day at her parents' home?

"In fact, it was not long after I got out of the hospital that I bought it for you. I didn't know what you would say or do when I came back here. But I bought it as a leap of faith. And I knew you. I knew you would wait, like your letter said. So I decided to take my own leap. And I prayed—'God, if You can make this come to pass, I will be the happiest man alive. If not, I'll know it is Your will.' But I trusted you, Lucy. I knew you would wait for me. You are the most honest and devoted woman there is."

"But why did you leave the other night?"

He blew out a sigh. "I wanted to wait for the right time and place to give you the ring. I'm sorry if it seemed like I was abandoning you. But I wanted to give this to you all along."

Lucy ran her finger over the small diamond set in a silver base.

"I love you, Lucy. Please forgive me for any hurt I've caused you. For not being there. But I will be here for you. Always. All I want to do is spend the rest of my life with you. . . ."

She gazed at the ring, thinking how perfect everything seemed here, with the river running by her feet. When she slipped the ring on her finger, he laughed as his arms swept her up in a tender embrace.

"Glory be," he murmured, nuzzling his face in her hair. "And you will have a whole man, Lucy. I promise."

"I have a whole man. His name is Nick Landers. He's more whole than any man there is, because God is with him."

Nick kissed her and then took up his muffin. "Now I'll have my end of the bargain." He bit into it. "Excellent as always, Lucy. Just as I remember. And that's all I remembered, even when I was over in Italy. I'd be in my tent, listening to the enemy fire and thinking of you and the times we had.

Wondering what you were doing. Hoping and praying that if I survived, God would somehow reunite us. And I'm glad He's faithful or I'd be one miserable and lonely person, knowing I might have lost the best woman in the world for me."

Lucy sighed. At that moment everything else faded but the man sitting before her and the miracle that God had wrought. Her tears began to flow. Tears from all the time spent waiting and wondering. And now to this special moment, with a ring on her finger and the promise of a man who wanted to spend his life with her.

"Are you okay, Lucy?" Nick asked, curling his arm around her.

"Yes. I'm just so happy."

ⷶ

Eight weeks later, Nick and Lucy stood before the shadow cast by Seneca Rocks in the green pasture and celebrated their marriage with family and friends. Nick stood on two legs for the ceremony, having obtained a prosthesis. Lucy wore her mother's wedding dress and her grandmother's pearls. The ceremony was simple but everything Lucy had ever dreamed it would be.

When the wedding ceremony concluded, everyone headed back to the Blands' home where Momma and Daddy put on a nice reception in the backyard, complete with plenty of miniature muffins and, of course, a wedding cake that Momma made from scratch. Lucy and Nick chatted with friends old and new. Just then, a shy man ventured forward. He sheepishly shook the hand Nick offered.

"You probably don't remember me, Captain Landers," he said slowly. "Sergeant Matthew Stacy. I was a private when we met. I liked this place so much I came back here to live after the war. And I became friends with Lucy's brother, Carl."

"Private Stacy," Nick repeated, his eyebrows furrowing. "I don't know. . ."

"I was one of the men you were trying to get to climb those rocks there. In fact, I told you it couldn't be done. You were gonna take me and Private Alexander on another climbing route to help us get over our fears when that man came and socked you in the face."

Nick nodded. "Oh, yes. I remember you now."

It was then that Matthew brought out a medal. "I want you to have this, sir. I guess you could call it a wedding gift. But this really belongs to you. You gave me the courage to make it up those rocks, even when I didn't want to. You know, after that incident at the rocks, I climbed them without any difficulty. I guess it was the idea of seeing an enemy attacking you that got me going. There was no more fear. And because of your training, I was able to help a few fellow soldiers get up those cliffs when we were in Italy. They gave me this medal."

"You keep it. You earned it."

Matthew shook his head, pressing the medal into Nick's hand. "No, sir. You earned it, for all of us. Please."

Nick slowly took the medal. Lucy could see his lips trembling and tears glazing his eyes. "Thank you. This means a great deal to me."

"I was sorry to hear about your leg. And about Sergeant Watkins. I know, and many of the privates agreed, if you hadn't done the training you did here, we couldn't have been victorious in Italy. And more of us would have died. Thank you." He shuffled off then and disappeared into the crowd that had gathered.

"Oh, Nick," Lucy said in wonder, gently rubbing a circle of comfort on his back as he stared at the medal in the palm of his hand. "God is so good."

Nick sniffed, drawing a finger over his eye. "Yes, He is all good, Lucy. All good."

She kissed him on the cheek and turned, only to find Allen staring at her. She froze. "Allen, hi. Thanks for coming."

"Lucy. I—I wanted to thank you for inviting me and Susan to your wedding. It was a real nice wedding."

"Thank you, Allen."

He hesitated. "And I just wanted to say—look, I know it's long overdue, but I want to apologize for hitting you that day, Captain, sir."

Nick looked at him in surprise.

"I mean, it was wrong of me. I see now that God has His plans for everyone. They just weren't my plans. And I'm glad we have stayed friends, Lucy. My wife, Susan, could use a friend, too. She doesn't know a whole lot of people around here."

"I'd love to get to know her, Allen," Lucy said. "Tell her to come over so I can meet her."

"She had to leave early. But here's a gift that she made for you."

Lucy took it with a trembling hand. She fought to steady it even as she undid the wrapper. It was a sampler with their wedding date and a message: *I can do all things through Christ who gives me strength.* "Thank you so much, Allen. I will treasure this always."

He scuffed his foot in the grass, then meandered off.

Lucy turned to see Nick looking first at the medal, then Allen, and finally the rocks of Seneca. "This is a day of miracles," he murmured. "Who would have thought?"

"God knew that this would be a day of miracles. And reconciliation."

"And a day when those who were separated are united forever as one. Right, Mrs. Landers?"

"Forever, my dear sweet Captain."

Lucy stood on her toes for a kiss that she gladly gave with all her heart.

A Letter To Our Readers

Dear Reader:
In order that we might better contribute to your reading
enjoyment, we would appreciate your taking a few minutes
to respond to the following questions. We welcome your
comments and read each form and letter we receive. When
completed, please return to the following:

Fiction Editor
Heartsong Presents
PO Box 719
Uhrichsville, Ohio 44683

1. Did you enjoy reading *Seneca Shadows* by Lauralee Bliss?
   ❏ Very much! I would like to see more books by this author!
   ❏ Moderately. I would have enjoyed it more if

   _____

   _____

   _____

2. Are you a member of **Heartsong Presents**? ❏ Yes ❏ No
   If no, where did you purchase this book? _____

   _____

3. How would you rate, on a scale from 1 (poor) to 5 (superior),
   the cover design? _____

4. On a scale from 1 (poor) to 10 (superior), please rate the
   following elements.

   ____ Heroine   ____ Plot
   ____ Hero   ____ Inspirational theme
   ____ Setting   ____ Secondary characters

5. These characters were special because? _____
_____
_____

6. How has this book inspired your life? _____
_____
_____

7. What settings would you like to see covered in future
   Heartsong Presents books? _____
_____
_____

8. What are some inspirational themes you would like to see
   treated in future books? _____
_____
_____

9. Would you be interested in reading other **Heartsong
   Presents** titles? ❏ Yes   ❏ No

10. Please check your age range:
    ❏ Under 18   ❏ 18-24
    ❏ 25-34   ❏ 35-45
    ❏ 46-55   ❏ Over 55

Name _____
Occupation _____
Address _____
City, State, Zip _____

Heart♥ong

Any 12
Heartsong
Presents titles
for only
$27.00*

HISTORICAL ROMANCE IS CHEAPER BY THE DOZEN!

Buy any assortment of twelve *Heartsong Presents* titles and save 25% off of the already discounted price of $2.97 each!

*plus $3.00 shipping and handling per order and sales tax where applicable. If outside the U.S. please call 740-922-7280 for shipping charges.

HEARTSONG PRESENTS TITLES AVAILABLE NOW:

(If ordering from this page, please remember to include it with the order form.)

Presents